Three Months To Change

Dinah Roseberry

Visionary Living Publishing/Visionary Living, Inc.
New Milford, Connecticut

Epigraph

Despite the lack of empirical support, electromagnetic energy in the brain may somehow interact with electromagnetic energy in the environment leading to unusual spontaneous events, sometimes thought to be paranormal, but more likely to be caused by one's own personal power to interact with the multiverse.

—Professor Frank Malone

Chapter One

HER HEAD ROCKED TO ONE SIDE, her neck cracking, and she could clearly taste a liquid copper residue in her mouth. He'd drawn blood at her lip. Again. And she was seeing stars this time. Well, not stars, per se, but pinpoints of light on a black backdrop interrupted by the tiniest of flickering dots.... The open-hand slap against her skin was hot, and it hurt like hell.

Wow, am I ever going to have a headache. If I even live through this. He wants to kill me this time. He probably will.

She knew her mouth was split open and the right corner of her eye was swelling shut. And her neck felt broken—she knew it probably wasn't because she'd have already been on the floor, but that didn't dispel the pain. The stars were *behind* her eyes, and she was pretty sure he'd hit her hard enough to take her consciousness from her. She'd be on the floor in a few seconds. And he'd be inside her home, bringing to mind Jack Nicholson with a knife in his hand at a snow-impacted hotel in Colorado. Jack's was a crazy laugh. Everyone hearing a laugh like that knew it. Everybody hearing a laugh like that took a step back. Quickly. Rocket science not required. *Get ready to go down*, she told herself, hoping that too much blood wouldn't damage the wood foyer. She'd hate to lose her security deposit.

But no. Something odd. A strength she knew she wasn't capable of jumped into her personal space. It was like electricity where none could possibly be. It was like a fire in the brain. It was like a rising from the ashes when there were no ashes—just a puddle of mush of what was left of her on the floor. The stars disappeared, but she could still hear the smug, crazy laughter coming from her gorilla of an ex-boyfriend.

Can't he take a hint, for God's sake?

He stood there at her door, halfway in her apartment and halfway on the porch. His laughter was sinister, and her flesh crawled with tiny prickles sticking her skin enhancing the feeling of *wrong place, wrong time.* Those prior blond good looks and intense blue-gray eyes that he'd used initially to subdue her were no longer attractive. In fact, they brought bile to her slender throat.

It hadn't taken her long to figure out that he was one of the worst men alive—especially in *her* life—but she suspected he'd brought pain to any relationship he'd touched. This was not new behavior for him. It *had* been for her, though. What had she seen in him? Since everything was moving in slow motion now—she'd heard of that happening, but had never experienced it before—she began to count off all the signs she'd ignored. There were plenty. And there would be time to think about it in this new, slowed-down world. Was this what they meant about seeing your life flash before your eyes? Was he really going to kill her? Yes...

But suddenly, there it was again. That strength. In her heart. In her mind. Clarity and crystal-clear thought processes. She pulled her face back around to confront him, her neck feeling like it had been ripped open from the impact he'd used when he'd slapped her. She was still standing—a surprise. His hand was raised to hit her again—backhanded this time. Those knuckles would hurt worse than the open hand, she was sure, especially with the ring he always wore. Her heartbeat sped up, and the fear of the next attack rushed to her brain. It was coming, it was coming…The strength took over again, calming her, slowing her heartbeat, exorcising the fear. It was as though something had stepped inside, or in front of, her small frame to take over when she couldn't cope. (Was she becoming schizophrenic? She'd seen on television that people with that disorder had multiple personalities, and sometimes those entities inside the mind took over. Was that was this was? Had he driven her mad? That was very possible.)

This jerk is a punk, she heard her mind say. Yet she frowned because though it had been *her* voice in her mind, the thought didn't really come from her brain somehow. *Schizophrenic for sure*, she thought before the upcoming face-off.

But no more thoughts came. Instead, she could feel the thinnest of a barrier enveloping her body, protecting her, shielding her from whatever was to come. Whatever it was allowed her to change her stance to solid, knee-bent positioning on the floor, left foot forward, right one behind to the right, angled and behind the left one. She knew her eyes were wide, and she was no longer focusing on Gorilla Ned. She could see his flashy white teeth and ominous blue-gray eyes all right, but she was looking at them through a kind of clear film that hugged her body—an intelligent film. Without further thought, she'd balled her right fist and struck out toward his face.

He blocked the hit with his wrist and bellowed laughter.

Before even a second passed, she felt her left fist ball and saw it come up fast with an uppercut to his jaw. That not only surprised him, but it broke his jaw, dropping him back to the porch floor.

She felt herself being pulled back one step and watched her door slam—him on the outside, her on the inside. The film dropped from her body, and the intensity left her mind. She stepped forward and dead-bolted the door.

Wow. Now that *was friggin' bizarre. What the hell just happened?*

She looked down at her hand: It should have been bruised, or cut, or at least hurt. But there was no pain at all. It was weird; how had she even known to hit him like that? The adrenaline was still pumping as she sucked in her breath and let her hand fall to her side. Calmness again came to her, feeling like a hug. Her own voice inside her head again came forth. *Call the police. Now. Before he does.* She looked at the coffee table where her phone had been, but it wasn't there. Looking down, she found it in her other hand. *What? How?*

Make the call now, her own voice said from inside her brain.

Turning from the cash register, Lenora saw herself in the mirror over the counter. She had a black eye, already a bit purple with green at the edges. She'd dressed that morning to match the eye because everyone would be looking at her. It would be an attempt to find humor in a despicable story. They probably wouldn't really notice the cut lip because the swelling had retreated, but the eye? Oh, yeah, people would be staring. She'd already decided what she was going to say. *Oh this? It's nothing. You should see the other guy.* Everybody said that, didn't they? Then change the subject. Cliché as it was, people would get the idea she wasn't going to talk about it. At least the Gorilla was out of her life for the time being, *if* the restraining order really worked. There was, of course, doubt on that account. She'd move on with her job—selling frames, displaying her artwork along with those frames, and being generally a really sweet girl.

Lenora sighed. She hated being known as sweet, but that's what she always got. She'd accepted it. In three months she would be 25 and she'd been called sweet for at least the prior ten years. Never sexy, or alluring, or beautiful. *Sweet.* The comments ranged from her sweet smile to her sweet stature, to her sweet eyes, to the sweet personality. Lenora shrugged. Sweet was good.

Something suddenly caught her attention outside the storefront glass. It was a blur, but then, as she looked straight on and out the sunny window, she saw a man. And not *just* a man. He was sexy, and alluring, and beautiful. Maybe *he* was sweet, too. She laughed under her breath, smiled at him, and then looked down at the invoice before her. Nothing good ever came from staring at a strange man—regardless of his attributes. If that had been one of her lessons she'd been sent to Earth to learn, well, Gorilla Ned had taught it to her very well. It was probably the sun shining through the window that illuminated him anyway. No one was that cute. And hadn't she just learned a lesson of the worst kind? Still, she tried to position her head just so, in an effort to see if he was still there, without him knowing she was making that effort. It was difficult to focus on him unless looking right at him, which she couldn't help but do again. This time he smiled back at her. She glanced away in a shy jerk of the head, ignoring the speeding up of her heart. When she looked back, not more than two seconds later, he was gone.

"Hmmm. *Poof*," she whispered. "Story of my life. Probably a serial killer anyway. My luck, these days."

The rest of the day at Framing Connections went on in a normal and characteristic fashion. She'd been working there part time for nearly a year. A customer before an employee, she knew as much about framing as any of the other clerks. She'd used the shop to frame her own abstract paintings for at least three years. When an opening came up, she'd decided to make an offer to them: She would work at the shop two to three days a week, counseling people about framing and of course selling frames. She would display her work for sale at a reasonable rate and give twenty percent commission of the sale to the shop.

She knew she was paid more than the other clerks because of her experience with framing and art, but reality told, she really did not do that much extra work to warrant the salary. Still, most of her income came from the sale of her paintings. They were fairly good—nothing special at this time in her career, but having the artist there and the customer seeing her "passion fire" often tipped the sale in her favor. She would be a force in the art world someday. When she was ready. Everybody said so. That and a dollar would get her a plain coffee with no trimmings at any fast-food joint. Maybe.

Just before the end of her shift at four, a flower delivery person entered. "Miss Lenora Dale?"

"That would be me," she said with a frown. "Flowers?" She squinted and pursed her lips. She bet the flowers were from Gorilla Ned. Didn't any of those jerks read the psychology books? Didn't they know most women were well aware that the flower gesture after a fight was just that—a gesture? And this was quite a bit more than a fight. It was assault. He wasn't going to change, the apology wasn't the truth, and she wasn't that stupid. He could send a full-grown oak tree and she would not feel any different. She casually touched her eye. *No, nothing's going to work this time, pal. I've learned the lesson. I'm moving on to whatever's next.*

The delivery boy didn't look to be over 16. "Flowers for a lovely lady," he said, showing a face full of white teeth in a smile so wide, some would say it was comical. Clowns came to mind. But not the evil kind.

"Thanks." Lenora's tone was flat. Then, "Wait, I want to give you a tip."

His smile became brighter (if that was possible). She had to grin inside. Just because she was in an "I hate all men" mode, didn't mean she had to be rude to a fellow worker bee. She pulled a five from her purse beneath the counter and handed it to him as he set on the counter not the expected bouquet but a plant with purple blooms in a matching purple container. With the five in hand, the boy made a quick exit. She pulled the tag from the dirt to see what kind of plant it was before she bothered with the card.

Aconitum. *Also known as Wolf's Bane.*

"Wolf's Bane? He's sending me Wolf's Bane? That's poisonous." She paused, pulling the card from its stick holder. "Figures the Gorilla would send me poison." She opened the card, ready to read, tear up, and drop it in the trash can. Instead, she read:

Miss Lenora Ellen Dale:

Your presence is requested at the reading of the last will and testament for Sir Wellington Bradley on this Friday coming at 10am. You have been identified as an heir to the estate due to a short relationship between your mother, Eileen Christine Dale, and Wellington Bradley with your birth as the result. A limousine will pick you up at your place of employment at 9am on Friday. Should you choose to forfeit your inheritance rights and refuse to attend this reading, please find this correspondence as formal notice that after your 25th birthday (in three months' time), all desired help will be refused.

Sincerely,
Johns and Johns, Esquires
Attorneys for the late Wellington Bradley

Lenora stood there, her mind spinning. Her mother had died from cancer the prior year, and the only thing she'd ever said about her father was that he had been a soldier and had been killed while on a secret mission before Lenora had been born. The odd thing was that on her deathbed, she'd said to Lenora, "I want to tell you something I haven't told you about your father before I go." Then she had promptly died. The death *and* birth of a mystery.

So what was this? Turning over the card and then looking at the envelope, she tried to discover some other clue. But she knew how this went. She'd call the florist and they would give her some nondescript answer advising that they did not know who or where or why. Still, she picked up the phone to make the call. Friday was only three days away.

Lenora was still thinking about the strange plant delivery as she walked along the running path that lined the lake near her workplace on her way home that afternoon. A light breeze ruffled her long, reddish-blonde hair pulled back in a low ponytail. Water glistened sunshine as she noted the small rowboats floating about. Sitting on a bench overlooking the lake, she took a deep breath of fresh air. How could a day like this, in a locale like this, have any kind of mystery attached to it? She had a *nothing can go wrong* feeling, even though just moments before there had been a gnawing intuition that something was about to happen that would change her life forever. She'd released that thought and just stared in contentment at the rippling water.

"Hello Doll," a voice said, uncomfortably close to her, making her jump and suck in her breath.

It was him. It was the lovely, wonderfully sexy man she'd seen looking in at her at the Framing Connections window front. But where had he come from? He'd certainly not been there just a moment before. Her eyes were wide as she studied him in the seconds it took for him to repeat his greeting. Had she picked up a stalker, somehow?

"Hello, Doll… I was just passing by and saw you sitting here. I've seen you at the framing shop in town just this morning."

Her voice left her, not so much because he'd popped out of nowhere but more because of his appearance—his dark brown eyes and hair. His clothing, however, was unusual for this day and age: He was dressed all in brown with cuffed pants (were they in style?) and a tan shirt and chocolate tie with a matching vest and jacket. Men just did not look like this in her experience. She was used to men in jeans and sandals, sometimes a shirt, sometimes not. This was that kind of town. Three-piece suits didn't happen in her world. He looked like a teacher.

"Yes," he said. "That's mostly right."

Lenora frowned. Had she said something? No, she hadn't, but she'd better because she was beginning to look like a deranged woman on a bench with wide eyes and an inability to make any kind of sound.

"Hello..." she said slowly, discomfort in her tone. "You called me Doll? I'm nobody's doll."

"Sorry, Doll; oh, sorry again—habit. You looked in such deep thought." He slid a bit closer on the bench, close enough to make her uncomfortable—not in her personal space, but nearly so.

"I did see you this morning and then you seemed to disappear. You should've come inside. We have quite a nice business if you're in need of framing."

"Or very good art, I'm told," he added, again flashing a smile.

Lenora blushed a bit before glancing into his eyes. This was all so unnatural. It seemed as if she were drowning in his gaze. His smile was so calming and she felt so relaxed. Calm and relaxed...Suddenly, her phone rang and she snapped her attention away from his hypnotic eyes. Glancing down at her purse, she pulled her phone from the inside pocket. She noted that a full hour had passed since she'd taken her seat on the bench. *An hour? How could I have been sitting here an hour?* The phone stopped ringing and she merely dropped it back in the purse without even bothering to slide it into its slot or see who was calling. It was not important somehow. Nothing was, except this exceptional man before her.

"Now, where were we?" he asked her just above a whisper, leaning forward and brushing back a strand of hair that had loosened itself from her ponytail.

She pulled back, stammering as she looked about her uneasily. "Well, I don't know, I seemed to have...spaced out or something."

He smiled again. "You'd just finished telling me about the time when you were 15, and you and your mother had gone hiking in Gettysburg at Devil's Den. You'd fallen and busted open your knee. We'd finished that story and you were about to tell me more of your thoughts about the reading of the will on Friday and how you thought your mother must have hid a very big secret from you."

Well, haven't I told him *the story of my life,* she thought flatly.

"Uhmmmm," was all she could manage.

"Well, I'm sure," the man began, "that the reason you've told me about the will, is that you—"

"I don't even know your name or anything about you."

"Really?" he said with a laugh. "Who have I been talking to this last hour?" Then he frowned and she watched as his expression went from one of contentment to one of worry. "My name is Frankie. That's what my friends always called me. My parents called me 'Franklin' because they always used that name when I was in trouble. And I was in trouble all the time." He stopped for a moment. "You really don't remember talking with me and me talking with you?"

Lenora shook her head. "I don't know. Maybe I'm under more stress than I thought. I've had a bad encounter—a physical encounter—with my ex-boyfriend and maybe that...I mean, if what that note said was true, I've had a father for all these years that my mom lied about. Why would she do that? Maybe to keep me in good spirits in my youth, but now as an adult woman? What could this all be about?"

"You're right, of course," Frankie replied. "I've heard of this type of thing before. Your mind is on autopilot and taking care of two things at once. Like hypnosis. Hypnotized by the radio, yet still carving a wood piece."

"Hypnosis? Wood? Did you hypnotize me?" She kept her stare blank, but closely watched him with suspicious eyes. Who was this person, who out of nowhere, now seemed to be cognizant of very intimate details from her life? Details that *she'd* obviously given him.

"No, no, of course not. I'm not a hypnotist by any means. I *have* read a lot in my lifetime about many subjects. I've heard of a 'break,' if you will, during conversation in hypnosis, but I've never seen such a thing...exactly..." He glanced away from her eyes and down to his feet, his elbows resting casually on his knees. "It all has to do with misplaced energy. You need to harness energy so that you can always be in control of what is happening around you. You're going to need to learn that."

Lenora had not stopped looking at him. "What?" she asked. "Energy? What are you talking about?"

"Actually, what I meant was for you to pull your energy and all your resources together so that you can go to the reading of the will. You never know what you might learn. I'd be happy to tag along with you, if you're nervous about going." Frankie looked back up at her with the look of a helpful confidant. "I could wait in the car." He paused. "And I'd be there if you needed me."

Lenora stood, took a step toward the lake, and stared across its expanse. "Thank you, Frankie. You helped me make up my mind. I will go, but I won't need an escort." She turned to him and smiled.

"Good, glad to be of assistance, Doll—"

She gave him a scowl that involved all the muscles in her face. "And what did you just call me again?"

"Doll. Oh. Not that. The beautiful Lenora, with the bright blonde hair and the hypnotizing green eyes. I'm glad to be of help." Then he stood, too. "I have to go now. My energy is—that is, I'm quite tired for some reason."

At the sound of birds overhead, Lenora turned to the water to watch their antics. "I'm glad you stopped to sit with me," she said and then turned back to him. "It's been a pleasure—" But he was gone. *Poof.* Again. Looking up and down the path, the grassy landscape behind her, and then back to the lake, she mumbled, "How does he *do* that?"

Walking home to her apartment just under one-half mile from the framing shop, Lenora took her time, window shopping, chatting with those she knew from the town. She loved the small-town life, the intimacy of knowing everyone, understanding the intricate involvements that held each and every family, business, and person together. It was where she received her inspiration. True, most did not see her interpretation of abstract oils until she explained them, but that was part of the charm—to allow someone who otherwise would have no impression of the balances of the heart to actually come away with a scene, a feel, a love of art. Alanwood was such a town: the Mid-Atlantic at its best.

Her mind slipped back to Frankie as she walked, a strange man in many ways, but so appealing. She'd felt a pull toward him from the first moment. It was as though he had a hold on her soul and the ability to interconnect with her on a level not previously explored. It was nothing like the abnormal attraction she'd felt in the beginning for Gorilla Ned. This felt different. This felt light on air. This felt fun. But how could that be from just one meeting? And one she'd zoned out of for the most part.

She was passing the small ice cream shop now, situated on the other side of the street, and thought momentarily about ending her workday with a cold treat. She stopped quickly, though, when she saw Frankie inside the very shop she'd been considering. He was standing at the counter, gazing at all the flavors of ice cream. Was it a coincidence that she'd now seen him three times in one day? Looking at her watch to check the time, she thought again of his brown eyes and hair...his charisma. And of the missing time she'd experienced in the park.

Noting it was after five, she glanced back at the ice cream shop wondering what time the business closed. Frankie was no longer there. He wasn't on the street that she could see either, as she quickly looked around. *Poof*, yet again. Had she really seen him?

It's a good thing I'm not a private detective following him, because I'd be a poor one.

Lenora, deciding to skip the ice cream idea, set off again for home. Suddenly, she felt very tired and the idea of a nap was more appealing than the extra calories of a chocolate milk shake. It was as though she was zapped of her energy, an unusual feeling for her. Energy; there was that word again. Somehow that seemed important. She shook her head, not having a clue why, and moved again along the sidewalk.

Lenora lived in the bottom apartment of an old Victorian home. The basement (partially finished) and first floor were hers, as was the left-side country garden and yard outside in the back. A fence divided the back yard, so that the upstairs tenants could also have a calming outside experience when they chose. Currently, there were no other tenants in the house, so the old home felt a bit lonely and creaky.

The inside of her home was beyond delightful, though, with its small rooms that those in the past had used for varied venues. The owners had nicely restructured two rooms into one on the first floor for the living room, added a bathroom and a walk-in closet (that had formerly been a very small room). Just to one side of her cozy living room was another room that sported glass doors along one wall looking out into the living space via small window-paned double doors, giving it a quaint feel. Lenora used this room as her office and gallery. Two other rooms had been structurally connected, giving her a nice-sized bedroom that had an entrance into the bathroom from both the living room and the bedroom. A nice, tidy, but small, modernized eat-in kitchen (if two chairs around a tiny table counted as eat-in) was at the back of the house leading out to the covered porch and country garden. For the money, it was a steal. The elderly owners rented it reasonably to those they felt had the right demeanor, so they could find the very best people and then keep them.

She'd lived there for nearly three years and never had a bit of trouble. Until Gorilla Ned, that is.

Lenora shivered. "What was *that*?" she said out loud. "Felt like someone dancing on my grave." She looked around, but saw nothing in her living space that would give her an uncomfortable feeling. Walking aimlessly through her apartment, she tried to identify the reason for her discomfort. It felt as though she was being watched. Not just watched, however: watched by *lots* of people. The apartment was empty except for her, though, and such a consideration was way offbeat. "Interesting," she whispered.

Finding oneself alone in a safe and comfortable place had a great deal to do with being safe and secure as a person. Lenora was just that, and that made any unusual feelings of this nature something to carefully consider—not that she'd ever had feelings like this before. They were alien to her. All her feelings, good or bad, went to canvas in color and drama. The world came alive via her hand-to-paintbrush and paintbrush-to-canvas. Stopping in the bedroom before her bed, Lenora noticed the air was slightly cold and seemed mobile without the ceiling fan or air on. Further, the cooler air was unusual because this room tended to hold the heat. Great in the wintertime, but in the spring or summer, not so much.

A nap. That's all I need. The shiver came from me being tired, and so I just need to lie down for a few moments. Then I'll get up and do some painting. Lying down fully dressed, she pulled the lightweight bedspread from one side of the bed over her as though she were a papoose wrapped in warmth. In seconds she could feel herself doze off, and it felt so delicious to drop into that land of inner knowing. Something tickled her nose, and her cheek itched giving her a shiver again. Even sleep felt odd today.

Suddenly, she felt the same strength she'd felt the night Gorilla Ned had come by to kick the daylights out of her. *Hah! Turned the table on you, ol' Ned. Next time you'll think twice.* Sleep began to take her, though the strength, in an armor-like cover, tightened around her. It was alive somehow with an energy made specifically for her, or so it seemed. Then it softened into…something else. There was a warm, inviting tremor that started at her temples and moved down her body, exiting at her toes. *Oh, so nice; I'd like more of that.* And more did come. Two, three, four waves of a delicious stroking of her soul. The energy seemed to be both inside her and outside, as well. *Why have I never felt this before? It's criminal that I'm just now having this.*

And then things changed again and she felt tendrils of power—for that's the only word she could think of that could describe the warm waves of whatever it was sliding along her body. This time, though, they stopped at her collar and, like a lover, nestled there, blowing soft, warm air and nibbling at the sensitive skin at the crevice of her neck and the even more sensitive ears. A small moan left her mouth in real time, not sleep time.

In moments, the waves were at her breasts, as though the material of her clothing was not protecting her from physical contact. She felt the tendrils wrap around them— both at the same time. She could feel licking and sucking, and her nipples grew hard and taut. Then something cupped them like invisible hands, all the while the tips feeling wet and so very hard. She pulled in her breath: *Harder, suck harder,* came from her mind. And as though the invisible wave could hear her, suction on her nipples increased until she was writhing. But then the wave pulled back.

"No," she whispered. "More; please don't stop."

It was then that she thought she heard a chuckle in her mind, not her own voice but that of another. A man. Someone she recognized. But the thinking left as quickly as the thought came. The wave moved lower and her excitement began to rise, making her forget all else, suspecting and hoping for what would happen next.

A small voice that was her own inside her head had questions, though. *What is this? Who is this? How is it happening, and why does it feel so real?* Then small chittering sounds like white noise moved into her mind and she knew she needed to focus on the sounds. It was important somehow. So as the wave moved down, she followed the directions of the chittering. She spread her jeans-clad legs and waited for the next delicious assault. The tendrils did not disappoint. She could feel them at first lapping at her outer private area (inside her clothing), somehow wet like a tongue, but stronger, more in control. As it latched on to the place where her pure raw emotion came from, her body arched. Whatever it was liked her reaction and she could feel the tendrils slide up inside her, deeper than she'd ever felt anyone at that entrance. At the same time, she found there were also other tendrils and waves hooked to her breasts and other sensual parts, pushing and sucking and pulling. It was all happening at once, building her up to a climax that would surely kill her, it was so ravenous. And she desired it like nothing she'd ever wanted before. She wanted to shout out: *Yes, yes!*

As she was giving herself over to the luscious feelings, her head tilted to one side. She frowned—both in startled fear and because she did not understand what she was seeing. There was a scene in mid-air to the right of her bed, a place and time not of this place and time where she lived. It was like she was watching a movie. The tendrils continued, but they slowed, as though allowing her to experience what she needed to experience, what she needed to see.

Lenora saw another room, and there were two men in this room. They were dressed in formal, three-piece suits. One was seated at a desk using what appeared to be an older, computer-like typewriter device, *tapping, tapping, tapping* on the keys. Another man stood in front of him, but with his back to her bedroom. A supervisor, maybe? *Why, this is out of a time, a long time ago.... What the hell am I seeing?*

It was then that the standing man turned toward her.

"Frankie!" she called out.

Chapter Two

AT THAT, SHE SAT UP IN BED, waves and tendrils gone, still fully clothed, and there was no scene at the side of her bed.

"That was Frankie in the room," she said out loud, but then shook her head and hopped clumsily out of the bed, nearly tripping over the bedspread and her own feet. *I must be losing my mind. And what happened to me?* She pushed away the thought that wanted to erupt forth, that *needed* to erupt forth. Running her hands over her body to see if she was still wearing all of her clothing, her mind screamed for answers. But she didn't want to acknowledge the thoughts that were coming, even if they were just quick desire, or memories, or dreams. The thoughts came anyway. Could it have been Frankie providing the total bliss to her body? *No! Absolutely not! I'm here all alone, with no one here, and all alone. All alone, I say! I'm losing my mind. But I'm* alone! She stood in front of her bed, her face a block of horror.

Still stumbling, she raced out of the bedroom, slamming the door behind her. *No sense leaving any opening for whatever it was to get out into the living room area. What to do, what to do....*

"I know," she said out loud, "Margo."

Margo was her best friend, crazy as she could be sometimes with all the ghost-hunting gear and psychic-medium stuff. Yes, it was popular in the "real world," but her friend had been involved with the supernatural for at least ten years or more. Oftentimes, Margo would drag Lenora along on her hunts. She'd learned how to use all the equipment, interacted with all Margo's ghost-hunting friends, and basically just had a good time. It was serious to them, but to her it was just interesting. Like mass hysteria.

Hearing the ringing of the phone on the other end of the line, Lenora hoped Margo was home. It was mid-week and she didn't usually make appointments for ghost investigations until the weekends. On the fourth ring, just before going to voicemail, Margo answered.

"Hey! It's funny you're calling—well, not funny, but *funny*—I mean not coincidental because I don't believe in coincidences, because there are no such things—but I had this thing going off in my head that I needed to talk to you—or that you needed to talk to me, or just that we needed to talk, ya know?"

Lenora smiled trying to be empathetic to the rantings that often escaped her friend's mouth. Margo made life fun. It was she who was always there when help was needed, too. She'd one time punched the Gorilla in the face just for something he'd said that she didn't like. And truthfully, he really *had* deserved it. But who thought that such a small woman at five feet in height could have that kind of power behind her? This bouncy, short-haired brunette with fire blue eyes who would stop at nothing to protect her. It had been that way since elementary school, though Lenora tried not to capitalize on it too much in her adulthood. This, of course, was different. It was Margo's area.

"Hi, Margo," she said before her friend could launch into a topic. "I think I just had a supernatural experience. It's really got me rattled."

"Only a matter of time," said Margo. "I'll be right over."

"Well, there's no rush exactly; I was thinking maybe—" But her friend was gone. Pulling the phone from her ear, she looked at the display and shook her head.

She knew Margo was packing up her gear and heading right over. No ghost unturned, etcetera. No use calling her cell and trying to convince her that the weekend was early enough, because that wasn't how Margo's mind worked: No time like the present. And to be honest, the present really *was* a good time, considering the strangeness of her experience. Could she ever sleep in her bedroom again after this?

It wasn't long before Margo came bursting through the door with all her gear in tow—packed into a silver, full-sized rolling case. She deposited it next to the couch and pointed to Lenora to sit down.

Lenora sat and pointed to the glass of wine she'd poured her friend. *She* certainly needed wine, so her friend might want it, too. But at present, Margo just paced back and forth in front of the coffee table as Lenora sipped the beverage.

"Okay, let's hear it," she said in a stern voice. Her eyes were set and her mouth taut. She was in what Lenora called *Ghostmode*. "What happened? You know this was only a matter of time, right? You being my friend and all. Bound to happen. Things rub off. Happens all the time. Go ahead."

Lenora took a long swig of wine and then began. "Well, there's this full, other-time scene that was on one side of my bedroom a little while ago."

Still pacing, Margo encouraged, "And, and..."

"Well, that's pretty much it..."

"Yeah right," said Margo and then snorted. "I can tell on your face there's more than that. Out with it. I'm your best friend. You can tell me anything. No judgment here. And ghosts have agendas. Always remember that."

"Well, that's kinda enough, in my eyes. I saw a classroom-like scene with two men in it, one on an old, old computer-like thing, and the other one..." Lenora trailed off.

Margo stopped pacing and watched Lenora with squinted eyes. "The other one, what?"

"I think I know him, but it doesn't make any sense, and it had to be a dream, except that...well, except that it didn't *feel* like one."

"Could be astral projection," said Margo, now seated in a chair and drumming her fingers on the nearby end table. "Or dimensional travel. I don't think time travel. Only because, well, why you?" She paused. "You're still not telling me something."

"Well," began Lenora, taking another swig of wine, "I kinda was having a...a...well, sexual kind of thing, when I turned to see the men in the room." Her cheeks blushed.

Margo shook her head. "Why are you blushing with me? You do remember that party last year? Nothing should embarrass you after that. So, who was the guy, and do you think it applies as part of the supernatural encounter?"

Lenora shrugged. "I don't know who it was, or what it was. Just that someone was really rocking the boat. There was no person at all, just the arousal feelings.... And I was totally dressed. I'm losing my mind, aren't I?"

"No, Lenny. I'm not sure if the sex is part of the experience or not. That could just be a dream not related to what you saw. You see, when you are most relaxed is when people who are not part of a big encounter often see things. By big, I mean like when a bunch of us are investigating. You, here alone, and relaxed enough to doze off, could make it easier for you to see something."

"There's one other thing," said Lenora. "One of the men in the room, the one that turned around to look at me, was someone I've just met today. And have seen two more times since."

"Okay, this puts a crimp into things," she said, still drumming her fingers. "Either the whole thing is a dream, or something from the other side is screwing with you, or the person you met today really was the person in the scene you saw."

"Now, *that* makes no sense at all."

"It does if he's a ghost," said Margo with nary a frown. "Tell me about this man you've met."

Frowning, Lenora delved into the tale of a warm Wednesday afternoon and the ultra-expansion of her own belief system. As she told the story, she realized how much she wanted a plain explanation for the events of the day. They really didn't seem so exciting and bizarre looking back. She'd seen a cute guy looking in the window at work. This same fellow sat with her at the park and volunteered to go with her to the reading of a will on Friday. He'd said he had to leave and he did. Maybe she'd just imagined him at the ice cream parlor. And then she'd had a dream—a sexual dream—and he'd been there at the end merely because she'd been attracted to him. Simple as that.

Margo was back to pacing. "Do you think the will has anything to do with Frankie? Did he hypnotize you? Because it sure as hell sounds like hypnosis. People can do that, ya know. Right while you're talking to them. They can put you under, just like that." She snapped her fingers.

"And what about this 'will' thing, Margo?" Lenora's voice cracked a bit. "What's that all about? Do you think I should go?"

"I do. I'd like to come with, but I can't miss work on Friday. *You* should go, though. If for nothing else than to find out you might be a millionaire or something. Or that you were left something really cool. A legacy, I don't know, stuff. I'd go for sure."

"Yes, I *have* decided to go...and I'll be going alone ...except do you think I will be safe getting into a strange limousine when I don't know where I'm going or who I'm going to see?" Lenora had nearly convinced herself to go, but this was the one catch she could think of. "Don't people disappear that way?"

"Hmmm," mumbled Margo, "true, so true." Then louder, she added, "How about I put a bug in your clothing and then if you don't show back up, me and the team will come looking for you?"

"You can do that? You do spy stuff, too?" Lenora stared. "You never cease to amaze me, dear friend. Yes, you can bug me."

With that, Lenora pulled out a clean bra and allowed Margo to slice a space in the strap area where there was double material, to slip in a tiny GPS bug she'd pulled from her rolling ghost case. "Now, at least I'll be able to find you. Of course, if you're dead, that won't matter."

Lenora grimaced. "Dead? Thanks for that thought."

"Just kidding, but make sure your phone is charged, immediately find out the license plate of the limo, and text it to me right away. Then text me as you go, so I know what's happening. Oh, and you'll be carrying pepper spray." She pulled a small container from her purse and handed it to Lenora. "Wear a jacket, and keep it in your pocket."

Lenora looked at the ceiling in thought. "What if they say, no phones, and blindfold me or something?"

"You do, indeed, watch a great deal of television. You're not being kidnapped. Kidnappers are not that stupid to do something like this—and why would anyone want you anyway? You don't have anything. Still, if they ask you to do that, you should *not* go. Common sense and all," said Margo, turning to head for the kitchen. "Got any sweets?"

"Cake in the taker," Lenora replied, lost in thought. She didn't have a bad feeling about the reading of the will and all the intrigue around it. There was no sixth sense telling her not to go or to beware of the dead. Not like all the weird stuff that came with this dream or whatever it was. She shrugged and joined her friend in the kitchen.

Friday morning held a gray sky and the chance of thunderstorms. A perfect day to read a will and think of the dead. Why Lenora had agreed (to herself) that she would go was beyond her thinking and her usually traditional way of looking and handling day-to-day things. It was different from art inspiration. Still, at 9am, she stood at the end of her workplace's driveway waiting for the limousine to arrive. She didn't have to wait more than a minute, as a shiny black Lincoln Continental pulled up, and a driver with a monkey hat stepped out. She scolded herself for looking at him that way. The hat after all was traditional, and the poor driver couldn't help that he was forced to wear such a uniform—for the rest of his attire reeked of someone having lots of money and conceit enough to have their workers purportedly under their thumbs.

The driver was nice, however. *Good sign for this not being a kidnapping.* Of course she could have taken that thought all over the place in a positive or negative direction. There was no time at present, though, because the driver was talking to her.

"Hello, Miss Dale. Not a pleasant day, but we'll be nice and dry in the car." He opened the back door for her.

Lenora began to get in, but stopped. "Oh wait," she said quickly, "I have to do something." She quickly stepped through the puddles that lined the street, splashing dirty water onto her jeans, and moved to the back of the car where she took a snapshot of the car's license plate, and then hit send to Margo. *Well, that is that, at least.*

"Ready, Miss? Anything else you need to do? I can give you the address to where we're going. It's not a secret now that you're here and attending the reading of the will. The secrecy was only in place if you'd chosen not to go. He handed her a card that showed the Bradley crest (she assumed) and the address of the home. Lenora snapped a photo of that as well, and sent it to Margo.

Margo replied in kind: *You go, girl. Please become a millionaire and then remember I'm a high-maintenance friend and require money to live the dream. Call me when you get back.*

The drive to the property, located some twenty-five miles outside of town, was pleasant, even though dim and damp circumstances surrounded her. The car ran smoothly and she felt no bumps or road mishaps. It was nice to ride in such an expensive car. The driver offered her drinks, snacks, and the ability to watch television. All interested her, but she chose to remain quiet, just looking at the scenery that flew by as they drove.

It wasn't long before the Lincoln turned into a very well-manicured drive with beautiful trees lining the way. These served two purposes: There was the aesthetic reason for looks, of course, but Lenora also noticed that at about every other tree cameras were mounted, aimed at the paved drive. This, then, would be a place well-protected from the outside world. Moving along the drive, slower now, she could see lovely gardens, topiary, and other treatments of plant and wildlife meant to offer a safe haven for all lucky enough to belong on the property.

Birds were everywhere despite the drizzling rain, and though they could easily escape by just flying away, she could see varieties that were very expensive and even so seemed to have no intention of leaving. It had to be due to food or other things, she guessed. There were also the regular variety of squirrels and deer munching at the distant edges of the property on the east side of the road that appeared to butt up to a forested area. May was a beautiful time for this location, she was sure, as the flowers were blooming and the foliage was a rich green. *What a place, even on a gray day.* It took everything she could do not to press her nose against the car window to take it all in like a child.

What if I am beneficiary of someone in all of this? How fantastic to paint here.

There was a rounded driveway drop-off that led into the front entranceway. The driver stopped and came around to open her door. He pointed to the few steps up to large wooden doors and said, "Have a nice day, Miss Dale. I'll be here when you are ready to go back home."

"Thank you," she said and then paused because she hadn't even asked his name. "Uhhmm..."

"Carl," he said, smiling. "I'll be right here."

She smiled back and then walked up the steps to knock on the massive door. The door swung open but no one was visible. She stepped inside out of the weather.

The foyer was large, but not as overpowering as she may have thought. This was not the typical mansion by any means. Once inside she noticed that what furnishings were there were grand, but the home felt stark. There were no carpets, and there were three doors off the foyer, all seeming to be steel plated—or some other kind of silver metal. They looked heavy, like those she'd imagined of the Middle Ages. She wondered what was behind such sturdy framework and whether she had made a mistake after all. It wasn't exactly that she had a negative feeling; it was just that what she was seeing from the lonely vestibule was not what she'd expected. There was almost a feeling that if she walked through any one of the steel doors, there would be something on the other side that would change her life forever—and maybe not for the better.

Now just where *are these thoughts coming from?* she mused as she continued to look around.

There was a lovely chandelier—very old, from the '40s or earlier, perhaps—situated two stories up, as this foyer also led to a simple staircase to a second floor. A walkway was directly in front of her at the second-story level so that someone might watch, from a distance, anyone who entered through the front door. And there indeed was someone—if you could call a bright orange-and-white-striped cat someone—staring out from between the railings at that higher level. She blinked, its size startled her so. This cat was as big as a dog! *Who has a cat that big? Talk about hormones or overfeeding...*

It was very interested in her and kept moving from between one railing to another to get a better or different view.

"Hello there," she said softly, if not nervously, looking up at the cat.

With that seeming invitation, the cat bounded to the staircase and flew on fast, fluffy legs down to her, standing then right in front of her, as if to say, *"Here I am; now we can begin our conversation."*

Lenora was game. "I'm supposed to be waiting for someone. Would that be you, sir—or madam?"

The cat answered with a long and loud meow.

Great, a talking *cat, no less.*

It came to wrap itself around her legs with the loudest purring she'd ever heard. She leaned down to scratch the cat's head as it rubbed its body against her and pushed its face into her hand—as cats will do. Lenora loved animals, though she did not have one of her own. She felt that her hours away from home precluded taking care of such a being in the right way.

Suddenly, one of the steel doors opened and a middle-aged man (dressed to the nines) walked out. He offered his hand to Lenora to shake.

"I'm Anthony Johns, Esquire, the late Mr. Bradley's lawyer. I see you've met Rex."

This last part about the cat held a tinge of disgust in his voice as if this cat was of poor upbringing and a nuisance to all living creatures.

Rex the cat merely turned his head away from the lawyer as if dismissing him.

Good form, thought Lenora, not a particular fan of lawyers. *Wow, I'm actually seeing body language from a cat.*

"Hello," returned Lenora. "I'm happy to meet you." *I think* was said under her breath. Then out loud, "A very lovely property here."

"Yes...I hope this visit will bring you some hope."

"Hope?" asked Lenora. "Hope for what?"

"Ah, well, that *is* the question isn't it?" he replied, giving a smirk with a small, superior-sounding laugh. The cat meowed and the lawyer rolled his eyes at the feline.

"This way, Miss Dale," said Johns, ushering her through the first door on the right.

Lenora followed as he pushed through a door that was heavier than she'd even thought it might be. "Why steel doors?" she asked as she moved into the next room.

"Oh, sometimes doors such as this are appropriate in a home, other times not; but the Bradley family is prepared for everything, of course. A stronghold for the worst of circumstances."

Perfect place to be if terrorism or apocalypse came about, she thought, giving the doors one last glance. Now her attention went to this new, massive room with its smattering of furniture around a fireplace. A long antique credenza sat to the left side of the space against the wall, and there were pastries, coffee, water, and another kind of drink—grape juice? To the right, a sectional sofa sat almost as if in its own living space, in front of a huge TV. The floors were bare, covered only with a type of linoleum. Scratched and battered linoleum. That was strange for such a lovely home.

Lenora didn't have much time to gaze about her because entering through a door at the other side of the room was a comely woman in her mid-50s, with hair so black it looked violet and eyes a cold, steel blue. She wore a dress that fell all the way to the floor and was made of brown brocade. Lenora swallowed hard. She'd not known this reading was a formal occasion, and thus her jeans, though starched and topped by a flora silk shirt and a linen jacket, was not on the same level as the outfit of this woman. *Could be just generational. Either way, I will not be intimidated by clothing.*

"Oh," said the woman, a touch of impatience in her tone. "You're early." Then she looked at the lawyer and said, "They always are, aren't they?"

The belittling tone angered Lenora. "I'm sorry," she said, looking directly at the woman's frightening, nearly dead, eyes. "The invitation said I was to be picked up at nine and brought here. If you have a problem with my arrival time, maybe you should take that up with your driver."

"Tsk, tsk, tsk. So touchy," replied the woman, now at the credenza pouring herself some of the purple liquid. "It's no matter. You may as well take a seat—and some refreshments. The reading will begin in about fifteen minutes. She turned, looked directly at Lenora and frowned. Without further discussion, she left the room by the same way she'd entered.

When Lenora turned back toward the lawyer, she found that he too had left the room. Lenora stood alone in the middle of the enormous room wondering what the hell she'd gotten herself into.

Going to the credenza, she poured herself some water after taking a quick sniff at the purple liquid: It smelled woodsy. What was it?

When Lenora turned back, there stood a handsome young man of about her own age or a bit older. His build was slim but muscular from what she could tell beneath his navy blue jacket and trousers. His white shirt was open at the neck and a jewel of some kind hung tightly at his throat. His hair was reddish-blond—more red than blond—and his eyes were hazel. He was very interesting to look at and hadn't verbally attacked her...yet.

"Hello, Lenora," he said jovially and with a big smile. He moved forward to shake her hand. "I've been looking forward to meeting another illegitimate."

Lenora tilted her head in question.

"Oh, not to worry. They won't call you that to your face, but you'll get the hint soon enough. Mommy Charlotte, who you just met in a manner of speaking, hates any of us who come to her home because of dear Daddy's infidelity. I join you on that long list. However, everyone, except you and I, have been booted from the family. Who knows what befell them? I hope you'll stay so that my drab life is not rooted among so many dogs." He laughed, and as he did, his eyes twinkled.

Lenora smiled. She liked him. But there was something about him—something cagy. And strange. It wouldn't do to let her guard down that quickly.

Others were coming in now from both sides of the room and they were all dressed as though the reading was a formal and festive occasion. Self-conscious, Lenora slipped to the side of the room away from everyone. The young man moved along with her.

"Don't be frightened," he said to her in a whisper. "Their barks are much worse than their bites." He paused to take a sip of the liquid from his glass. "Well, most times."

"I'm not afraid," she answered. "Just underdressed."

The man started giggling as though she'd made some wonderful joke, and Lenora shook her head, again questioning what this whole reading of a will was all about.

The young man leaned in again to whisper in her ear. "Don't let them scare you off. That's what they try to do so they don't have to acknowledge Daddy's 'loose,' as they call it, behavior. Believe me when I say that you will need us in the next three months and thereafter; you can't afford to get your back up. I can get away with it; I've been here four years. You? Barely an hour. The next three months will be the most important of your life. So be honest when you are asked questions. And hold your tongue so that Charlotte doesn't kick you out. That's what normally happens, you know. I'm the only one who's passed the tests." He tapped his index finger against his temple indicating to her that he was smarter than the others.

"Tests—" she began.

A loud voice boomed over her whisper. It was the condescending woman from before. "Excuse me, Miss Dale, maybe you'd like to share what you're discussing with Rex?"

The entire group of people was silent, waiting for her to speak. The intimidation was thick in the room as everyone stared at her with nary a welcome expression. She remembered what the young man had said about being kicked out, so she took a breath and blew it out to calm down. Then she frowned.

"Rex, like Rex the cat?" she asked, turning from the crowd to look at the young man.

That must have broken the ice, because everyone began laughing—except Charlotte. Rex the man just gave her a sarcastic smile.

"Everyone loves Rex the cat," began Rex. "Not so much Rex the man. I'm hoping to change that, however, with this new family member, Miss Dale." Then he began to clap his hands.

Slowly, and not before looking around the room, the others joined in—except for Charlotte, who merely glared at everyone else. She raised her hand to ask for quiet. "Well, Rex, we shall see what the day brings."

Her smile seemed to have a touch of evil, or maybe it was her stormy eyes, and she was merely a rude, middle-aged woman. Lenora had never seen such strange eyes, though; but as she looked around her, she found that everyone there was "different" and had eyes that she could not easily describe.

The lawyer finally stepped up to the front of the room and began his speech about the importance of wills, of having such a document to allow the significant moments and items to go on long after a death.

Lenora, after about ten minutes of a pep talk preparation to the will, was yawning and trying to stifle it. Whenever she glanced his way, she caught Rex looking at her. He was certainly enamored. *Mmmm, two handsome men in just a few days.* Her luck was certainly changing. However, she could not get the feeling of a disaster about to happen out of her mind.

Rex nudged her and whispered, "This is the part to pay attention to."

She nodded and turned to thank him, but he was gone. *Men just poof in and out of my life,* she thought in irritation. But she did look toward the lawyer and began to actively listen.

"The terms of the will are consistent with what most of us believed to be true. No surprise there. The home and entire property is left to—and I quote—my dearest wife and companion for over 400 years, Charlotte."

Lenora perked up. *What? 400 years? What the* hell?

"This home, property, and refuge will be maintained by the family and offer assistance, hope, and correction to those in need, regardless of formal family ties. That is to say that Rex shall continue to have refuge here, his own space to grow, and a commonality of familial companionship as all other family members. Miss Dale will have the opportunity to accept the same cordiality, but only after her 25th birthday, and be willing to continue her training in a manner that will move forward the family name. It will be her responsibility to seek assistance these next few months involving the beginning of her powers, and then after the fact—once 25—she must interpret and rely on herself to find her correct place within the family."

Then Johns looked directly at Lenora.

"If, Miss Dale, you choose to squander this inheritance, your training becomes moot, and you will be left to your own devices to foster a life outside the family's protection.

"Well, that does it, folks. Charlotte remains in charge and the only real change is the introduction of Miss Dale into the family, which I know there is a certain reluctance to have her."

Lenora spoke up. "I'm very sorry, but I don't understand any of this. I don't want to belong to your family. I don't want to live here, or be trained here—for what I don't know—or to take any of the intimidation that I clearly feel from all of you."

She glanced to her right and found that Rex was back, very close to her. "Hold your tongue, Lenora; don't get too persnickety. Back down," he whispered.

But apparently it was too late. Charlotte stood and walked directly to Lenora stopping about four feet from her. "Intimidation, you say?" she said in amusement. "How's *this* for intimidation?"

Suddenly, she moved to all fours, her dress tearing on one side where it was slit up to her thigh. A growl took over her voice, a time of fast movement and swirling air—so fast that Lenora could not see—and in seconds, there before Lenora was a wolf. Not just a regular wolf, but a creature so large and so frightening that Lenora fell back in horror. The last thing she remembered was looking up into Rex's eyes and hearing him say, "I told you to back down, Lenora."

Everything went black.

Chapter Three

AT SOME POINT, LENORA COULD SEE a pinpoint of light, and she began to come back to consciousness. It was a small, seemingly insignificant light that sent her along a tunnel back to her mind. Her brain told her this was something to fight. She mustn't wake up. Not after what she'd seen. She should go the other way along the tunnel, toward heaven, but that didn't appear to be in the plan.

Hugging the tunnel wall and trying to slow down, she thought about what had put her on this course. It could not have been real. It was like a movie, or a TV show, or a book. The thing she'd seen was a werewolf. At least that's what she knew popular culture to call it. And what could that mean? Did it mean that such things were not the fabrication of creative minds, but reality? Now that she was part of this family—at least that's what they had said—would she too turn into something like that? After all, that wolf woman's husband had been her father. She didn't know. Why would her mother hide something like that from her?

She just knew that she needed to repair her mind and stay down in the dark in the tunnel. She needed to convince herself that what she'd seen was not real. It was just some kind of hypnosis. That was it. Frankie—dear Frankie—had said: People could be hypnotized. Lenora sank back down into the depths of her consciousness and moved as slowly as she possibly could along the tunnel wall.

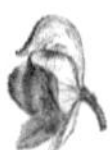

Lenora woke and stretched, finding herself in her own bed. *Wow, what a dream* that *was!* "What day is it?" she said out loud.

A nearby voice said, "Friday; it's Friday afternoon, Doll."

A voice in her house, in *her* home? She squinted at the sunlight coming through the window, trying both to wake up and to see who had spoken.

"Frankie?" she uttered and sat up in bed. She looked down to make sure she was still clothed—she was—and then back to him. "What are you doing here and how did you find me? I never told you my address." Though she was surprised and wary, at least someone was here to help her back from madness. *Yeah, right, probably a stalker. That's how my day is going.*

"Well," he began, moving to sit on the edge of the bed. "I'm ashamed to say that while I was out walking this morning, I happened by your shop as you were leaving in a limo. I'm not a stalker, I assure you, Doll. Then I remembered you were going to that will reading today. I went on my way, but decided to stop back a few hours later to see how things went. They gave me your address at the shop when I said we were friends. You don't mind, do you?"

Lenora shook her head, still trying to dislodge the cobwebs in her brain. His answer didn't reassure. He *was* stalking her. "No...no...but how did I get here? Who put me to bed?"

"Let me get you some water," he offered, and quickly left the room, headed for her kitchen.

The perfect stall while he thinks of a plausible explanation. How does he know his way around my house? Was he snooping while I was out like a light? None of this makes sense.

Coming back with a glass of ice water, cubes tinkling against the glass, he said, "I arrived just as your limousine did this afternoon. There was a driver and a man named Rex. Very nice sort, but odd and distrusting.... Anyway, you were unconscious—you'd fainted, I gathered from their talk—and I was very alarmed. Rex brought you in and put you on your bed. I followed along. All he said to you was, "You'll be okay, Lenny. You just had a scare. Everyone reacts that way the first time." Then he left.

"Did you ask any questions?" asked Lenora. "Did he tell you what I think I saw?"

"No, he was not obliged to even notice me. Very strong sort—he dismissed me like I was not even here." Frankie wrinkled his nose. "I'm not inclined to like him, if truth be told."

Suddenly, a very large orange-and-white cat bounced up on the bed, purring, and making its way to snuggle against Lenora. "Holy cow!" she said. "He left Rex behind." She petted the cat and fell into baby talk. "What are you doing here, you pretty baby?" The cat happily responded with mewing.

Frankie was frowning. "That cat is not Rex; the man is Rex. I heard the driver call him that."

"It's a long story, but—well, it's not that long, but suffice it to say that Rex the man, has a cat named Rex. Or the family does. I don't really know who owns the cat." She turned her attention from the cat and looked at Frankie, no longer feeling the stalker vibes. "But that's not the problem. It's what I saw."

Frankie sat quietly waiting for her explanation, his body seeming to tense, showing that he somehow knew that what was coming would not be good. He whispered, "I knew I should have gone with you."

"Tell me about it," she said, her tone touched with sarcasm. "I saw a woman turn into a wolf."

Frankie continued to sit still, his face blank.

"Seriously," she said. "I'm not making this up. I saw it; then I must have fainted; then I showed up here with you and the cat. And no memory of anything in between." She paused and attempted to lighten the mood. "Rex must have left his cat here to look over me—as you can see, he is very affectionate." She absently rubbed the feline behind the ears. "Or maybe he left him by accident. Or on purpose, so I'll have to return him...."

Lenora could tell by just looking at Frankie that he was having a hard time with what she was saying. But wouldn't anyone? There were no such things as women turning into wolves. She watched Frankie thinking and making decisions about what she'd told him. His brow was wrinkled now and his mouth taut. He wasn't buying it.

"What was the will about? What did it say about you?" he said, trying (she thought) to take her mind from the wolf story.

It worked to a point. What *had* the will been about? "Something about training and belonging there after my 25th birthday—which is in three months. I honestly didn't learn very much. The lady of the house—my newfound dead father's wife—became angry at me and then she wasn't there. A wolf was there and it looked like it was going attack me. And I know it was her because I saw her change in this fast kinda movement thing, and then the wolf had on a collar that looked exactly like her necklace. That's all I remember. And what about this cat?"

Frankie handed her the glass of water. "I don't think you'll have to worry about the cat. Rex will be back for his cat. Nobody leaves behind a beauty like this one."

But that wasn't the end of the story. She could tell by looking at Frankie that he knew something she didn't know. And for the life of her she could not understand how that was possible. Now he was looking around the room uncomfortably, his gaze falling on the wooden door to her basement.

"What?" she asked, trying to jar his thought.

"Is that your basement?" he asked, seemingly trying to be casual.

"Yup," she said, and then raised her eyebrows. "Why?"

"You should probably leave the door closed from now on." His voice was flat and he kept looking at the door.

"Why?" Lenora asked with a frown.

"Uhmm, well, Doll—"

"You did *not* just call me Doll again." Now it was her turn to have a flat tone.

"I'm truly sorry. I have such habits, don't I?"

Lenora shrugged. "So, what's with the basement?"

"Well," he began and then faltered before recovering to say, "The cat may need to go down there—you will need to fix up a litter box for him. And you don't want him dragging litter on his feet into your living room."

Lenora's eyes narrowed. He'd not been thinking about her basement for cat duties. There was something else he wasn't telling her. But what did any of this have to do with her basement? "Would you like to see the basement?" she asked.

He suddenly stood and looked directly at her, but it had been difficult for him to look away from the basement door. "N-no," he stammered. "That won't be necessary; I definitely do not want to see your basement." Then he seemed to catch her reaction, and changed his frown to a smile. "Basements are much too creepy for me." He laughed and then cleared his throat. "You'll want to keep the door closed, though ...because of the cat. I have to go now."

With that, he quickly headed for the front door and then turned to smile at Lenora. She pulled open the door for him and he walked out.

Lenora stood watching him as he left. "That was strange," she began, and then looked at Rex who was lounging on her sofa taking up two cushions. "What do you think of him, Rex? Quite cute, yes?"

Rex jumped off the couch and, as if to ignore her, ran to the basement door.

"Whoa, Nelly," said Lenora. "There's no litter box down there yet! I think the last people left some of that stuff in the hall cupboard to use for icy sidewalks."

But the cat was having none of the wait. He meowed at the basement door.

"What *is* it about this basement? There's nothing there but storage and my washer/dryer, and I don't want you hiding there. I've got other things to think about right now."

Rex pawed at the door and uttered low grumbling sounds.

"All right, already," Lenora said in exasperation. She pulled open the door.

But Rex did not go down the steps to the lower level. He merely peered down them, moving his head and body so that he could see as far as possible without stepping down the first step. Lenora, surprised at this behavior, also looked down the stairs. She reached out and flipped on the light switch just inside the basement door.

Just before—a millisecond before—the light beaconed the stairwell, she thought she saw a white mist. But in full light, there was nothing to see, and so her brain just let that millisecond slide away. She looked down at the cat, and the cat looked up at her.

"Looks like you have something to say about my basement," she said, stooping to pet him. "Nothing there, but I'll leave the door open just in case you need to go down. I'll fix up a box for you till your daddy comes back." Then under her breath she added, "Maybe he'll have some answers for me, because I couldn't have seen what I know I saw."

After saying that, she glanced down the stairs again. Had there been a mist? No. Imagination. But Frankie had seemed spooked. And now the cat's behavior…"Well, enough of this basement business. I'm going down there. I don't need to be scared of my basement on top of everything else." Down the steps she went, as Rex stretched his neck to see her turn the corner at the bottom of the stairs, without allowing his paws to touch the step. "Chicken!" she called back up to him, and mentally to the absent Frankie.

The light bulb that lit the lower floor was not bright. Even at full capacity, it barely gave more than a dim reality. She had not bothered about it before, as it was only a place to do her laundry or store whatever items that cluttered the upstairs living space: a few boxes, an old treadmill, and a bike (that she rarely used). The lid to the washer was up seeming to invite any shadows to jump in and be washed of evil or maybe just…this was silly. Nothing was in the basement. No evil and no mist. Rex and Frankie were just spooked because of her behavior and mannerisms after that strange dream of wolf woman. Or vision. Or whatever that was. But none of it really made sense, did it?

At any rate, she slowly scanned the basement from the middle of the floor when: *Bam!* A noise sounded, so loud it made her jump and her heart race. The washing machine lid had slammed down in a most harsh way. But how? No airflow, no wind. No people, no hands to slam it. So what had made *that* happen? She inched toward the washer when she heard another noise from the far corner of the room where the light barely penetrated. There it was. A milky-foggy-misty-cloudy thing. And it seemed to be getting bigger and bigger. Her ears strained because she thought she could hear the slightest whisper—or many whispers. The words, however, were not clear.

She pulled herself to full height and huffed. "Well, Margo will be pleased. I've got ghosts.... Ghosts, wolves, strange scenes, cats, and sex. What else could crop up? This is madness."

She was surprised that she didn't feel fear or some sort of emotion that would activate the fight-or-flight response. She just felt annoyed. "So, I'm going upstairs now, and I'd appreciate it if you didn't scare anybody. Especially me. I've got enough to worry about just now."

With that she stomped up the stairs and slammed the door behind her.

Rex was still near and she said to the cat, "We've got ghosts. Can you believe it?"

The cat's hair was ridged along his back as if to say, "Not good, not good at all."

"Not to worry," she soothed. "Margo will get rid of them. It's what she does."

"Get rid of who?" Frankie said from behind her.

Lenora jumped again. He'd come back and she'd not even heard him. What the heck was he doing back? She couldn't have men coming and going like this! As she turned, fear hit her squarely in the stomach. But then she calmed; Frankie stood very close. Handsome as ever. Making her feel warm and wanted. Sweet Frankie. But at the same time ... strange Frankie. Frankie who should *not* be here.

"You're back, I see. I thought you were leaving." She paused. "There are ghosts down there," she said an off-hand manner.

Frankie's body tightened and his eyes were wide. "You've seen them?"

"Well," she said with a frown, "I *did* see something, and it appeared that it wanted me to see it—or them. When they—or it—slammed down the washer lid, that scared the hell out of me. It was so loud!"

Frankie frowned. "I didn't hear anything. I was right here and didn't hear anything." He moved to the door, gently pushing it shut. "Even so, we should keep whatever is down there...well, down there, Dollface."

"Dollface now, is it? I don't like that any better than Doll. And why did you come back? Forget something?"

"No...just wanted to, had to, for some reason. And sorry about the doll names; it's a habit, as I've said." He looked squeamish.

"Ya know," she said to him casually, but keeping her eyes peeled for more strange behavior, "if it's ghosts, a closed door won't keep them down there."

"You'd be surprised," he said with a nod. "So surprised."

"So now you're a ghost expert, eh?" She watched him carefully, for he was definitely spooked. Maybe she wasn't spooked *enough*. There *had* been a mist after all.

"Oh, wait." She went to the door again to open it. "I don't see Rex. He must have slipped down there while we were talking."

She saw Frankie take in his breath sharply and look around the room.

"What?" she said and turned from him to the basement door. "Not really that afraid of a few little ghosts, are you?" That said, she was not that comfortable with the idea either, considering the things that had been happening of late.

When she opened the door, she noticed that the light was still on. She'd forgotten to turn it off, so she moved down a few steps. "Rex! Rex, are you down here?"

A voice came from behind her in her living room. "No, actually, I'm right here. What, pray tell, are you doing down there?"

She recognized the voice, and it wasn't Frankie. "Rex, is that you?" She quickly came back up the stairs. There in her living room stood Rex the person. She looked around for Frankie. He was nowhere to be seen.

"Did you see Frankie?" she queried him. "And where's your cat? He was here a few minutes ago, but I can't find him now. And how did you get in?"

"Not to worry about him. He's quite ingenious when hiding. And to answer your other question, there was no one here when I came in. Window's open though. Perhaps your friend fled for some reason."

"Fled? What are you talking about? Fled from what?"

"Or who, might be the better question." His eyes were merry, and he had a smug smile on his face.

"Yeah, right," replied Lenora with sarcasm, "and as I asked, how did you get in here anyway? Obviously, Frankie didn't let you in."

"No, actually the door was unlocked and I heard this loud bang and just decided to come in to see if you were all right. You didn't answer my knocking, you know. Damsel in distress and all."

"You heard the bang?" she asked, a frown touching her brow again. "Frankie didn't hear it. That's odd."

"Who is this Frankie?" Rex asked. "And why would he flee from me out the window?"

"I'm sure that's not what happened." She could not see her Frankie behaving in that way. *Her Frankie.* Strange as he was, she inwardly sighed, and a smile touched her lips. Frankie was strong and wonderful. Not the type to be spooked by someone. Well, maybe he *was* spooked—but of the ghosts. Still, the window? Please. She would have to take this disappearing act up with him. *Cute* did not excuse *weird.* Or rude. For now, she brought her attention back to Rex.

"Did you know your cat was here? He's been hanging out with me as though he were my cat."

"Good old Rex the cat," he answered and then laughed. "No telling what he'll do."

"Hmm." There seemed to be a lot of that going around. "Well, be that as it may, he's here someplace, and I'm sure he's ready to go home with you."

"Possibly," said Rex. Changing the subject, he said, "Have you given more thought to what happened at my stepmother's little house in the woods? Do you feel like Red Riding Hood?" He laughed again.

That moment brought fear to her again and gooseflesh traveled up her arms. That visit was not funny in any way. "I must have had a hallucination. What I saw can't possibly be real." She cleared her throat to dislodge the lump that had quickly taken over, choking her at the thought of the scene she'd witnessed. "I've undergone some kind of psychotic break or something."

"Oh, it's real, all right. Charlotte is a real *animal* in every sense of the word. You've heard the legends about werewolves, haven't you? Watched the movies and TV shows?"

Lenora brought a hand to her throat without thinking. "Of course, I have, but that stuff's not real. This was in-your-face, absolutely real—unless, like I said, I was seeing things."

"You weren't. This may be a rude awakening for you, I know, but I'm here to help. I'm not allowed to help, but I'm doing it anyway. We'll have to keep this off Charlotte's radar. And believe me, she has some pretty strong radar. But, if you have to go through this alone, you'll go mad, and they will disown you. That's what Charlotte wants. No reminders of dear Daddy's infidelity over the years. You can't afford in this day and age not to have family protection as a part of your life." He casually sat on the sofa. "Charlotte wants you never to come back. She wants you scared to death and in a mental hospital until you die from some self-inflicted suicidal mishap. And the will stipulates that if you don't come asking for help within the three months before you come of wolf age, that she can disown you. Like I said, she didn't like dear old Daddy having other...interests...and she'd rather see you dead as he is. Me, too, for that matter. She has my coffin all picked out."

Lenora's eyes went wide. Where was Frankie when she needed him?

She had no clue why she was allowing Rex to drive her back to that house of horrors. One hand clutched the door handle of his sports car, her white knuckles trying to pull her thoughts from the sharp twists of the road. She wished Frankie was with her. He'd offered before and she'd declined. This time she would have welcomed his rational thinking. Well, maybe it wasn't exactly rational, but he was a warm body to hold on to if the worst happened. But no, he was *poof* gone. And no phone…that was so odd. Everyone had a phone these days, but he had just pushed her inquiry off as so much societal flotsam. And she should have called Margo, too. Her mind was not working right.

Rex was talking, but she'd not been listening, feeling sorry for herself and terrified of what was about to come.

"…And that's all you really have to do," he was saying. "Hey, Lenny. You hearing me?"

Lenora crinkled her nose. "Everyone has a nickname for me these days. Lenora. No Lenny, no Doll. Only my best friend calls me Lenny."

"Doll?" he inquired, glancing at her quickly as he entered another sharp turn while going over the suggested speed. "Frankie again?"

"Yes," she whispered. "I wonder what happened to him…"

"Listen, you better stop thinking about him, and think about what you're going to say to Charlotte. She'll have questions, and you better have answers."

Lenora sighed hard. Not think of Frankie? That was the only thing that kept her from leaping out of the car to the hard pavement in an attempt to put herself into a hospital bed away from the madness of wolves. "Sorry," she whispered. "Frankie is my sanity right now. This is all nuts. I'm still not sure I saw what I saw, even though you say I did see it. What the hell, Rex?"

"We don't have time for a history lesson right now. That can come soon enough. Right now, what you need to know is that you have to ask her for help. You have to tell her what's been happening to you—the gorilla ex-boyfriend thing you told me about. And seeing things. If you don't ask for help, on the day you turn 25, you will be on your own. Trust me, you don't want to be on your own with powers or whatever else comes. The abilities are likely to kill you before you start to understand them. It's happened to everyone else in this same situation but me. Numbers don't lie or change in this family."

The road was smooth now, and Lenora allowed her knuckles to loosen on the door handle. She thought about what Rex was saying and quickly ran through what she would say to Charlotte. There was the force field around her when Ned had attacked her. And her phone had jumped into her hand...though she didn't really remember that— it was just there. And there was the scene from the past in her bedroom. She shook her head.

"What?" asked Rex.

"That scene into the past. That had to be a dream and not part of this, because Frankie was in it. I was dreaming." She sniffed and then added to herself, *At least I hope it was a dream because some invisible force was making love to me.*

"And what do you mean, it didn't happen to you?" inquired Lenora.

"Well, things happened—of that you can be sure. But, you see, all of us have been different. That is, those of us outside the royal blood line. They are total shapeshifters. That's not quite what we turned into... but you'll understand that soon enough. You've too much to take in right now with your own issues."

They went back to silence, both inside their own ideas of what was about to take place.

It was difficult to concentrate on anything Rex had said because her stomach was doing flips—and not the good kind. *What am I doing here? Okay, so there's a change coming. I'm not going to turn into a wolf like Charlotte. This is all madness, and I am imagining things.*

Lenora glanced to the left and noticed Rex was looking at her with concern as he glanced back and forth between her and the road.

"I just need quiet," she said, stopping him before he launched into another tirade about what to say to Charlotte. "I need to...gather myself."

Seeming to understand, he nodded and looked back to the road. The silence returned.

But Lenora's mind was not quiet. It was clicking off reasons to turn back. She'd come too far for that, though. *Relax*, she ordered herself. Interestingly enough, she did relax. Closing her eyes she saw Frankie in her mind. He was looking intently at her and stroking her cheek ever so softly. His fingers slid so softly on her skin that she felt she could feel her flesh quiver and tickle under the touch. His nearness calmed her in a way she'd not felt with anyone else. And she could tell by the look in his eyes that he felt the same. They were fated lovers.

"This will be the most difficult time, Doll," he said, "but you are powerful and smart. You'll be okay." His eyes peered deeply into hers and she saw a longing and desire that was unmistakable—it felt real. It felt like he was there in the car with her. She could smell his cologne and feel his touch. *How is this possible?*

"Lenora?" Rex said, breaking into her thoughts. "Are you okay? It seems as though you are barely breathing."

She blinked her eyes and Frankie melted away.

She sighed, sorry she'd lost the moment. "Yes. I think I was dreaming...."

"Well, we're almost there. Are you set in your mind as to what you will say to Charlotte? You have to treat her so carefully, dear one. Like royalty."

Lenora frowned. Cowing to this woman—wolf or not— was not in her repertoire of abilities. "Assertive," she said to Rex with a finality to her tone. "I'm going to be assertive."

"Hmm," Rex said barely above a murmur. "I hope that's something you know how to do well, or we're both in trouble."

"No, I won't drag you in, no matter what. I promise."

Turning into the long driveway from the other side of the woods, they again went back to their own thoughts. Lenora jumped as Rex reached to take her hand. He brought it to his lips and gently kissed her fingers.

Suddenly, it felt as though the air was being sucked out of the car. An energy so strong enveloped her, and when she looked at Rex, she could tell that he too was feeling the surge of power.

"Is that you?" he said, struggling with his breath and stopping the car. "Relax it!" he sputtered, his breath leaving his body just as hers was.

"It's not me," she answered, also finding it difficult to breathe. "At least I don't think it is!" To herself she shouted out, *Frankie! Help me!*

Then, just as quickly as the air left the car, the pressure normalized and the two were again able to breathe.

Thank you, Frankie.

"What the hell was that?" said Rex, looking at her with wide eyes. "Can you send the air out of a place? I've never heard of that power! Ha! Won't Charlotte be surprised when she can't breathe?"

"Yeah, great, if that was me. Then, as you can see, *we* lose air as well. I'm not in control—that is, if I'm the one doing it. It's a first, that's for sure." She allowed her body to slump with her head resting against the window. "Frankie," she whispered.

"Frankie?" Rex asked, shaking his head and rolling his eyes. "Is that was this is about?"

"No," Lenora snapped. Then to herself, *Why did I call for him like that? What's happening to me? Why is that connection so strong?*

"Snap out of it," Rex said loudly. "We're here, and it looks like several other members of the family are here, too." Then softly, "Figures."

Lenora didn't answer him, but sat very still looking absently out of the front window. She was hearing Frankie in her head. *I'm right there with you, Doll. If you concentrate, you'll be able to see me in your mind.*

She forced herself to relax and to breathe slowly in and out. Suddenly, there he was, standing in front of the car. He was wearing a lab coat of some kind. And he was so clear, she had to marvel at the power of her own mind. "Okay, I see you," she said, barely above a whisper. *Think I'm going to need you in there, so don't go anyplace.*

Frankie smiled, melting her heart. He said inside her mind, *Don't worry. I'll be right there. You just have to look around the room to see me.*

Lenora cleared her throat and stretched her arms. Turning to Rex, she said, "I'm ready."

Rex seemed uncertain. No doubt, he'd heard her quiet musing to Frankie. Well, that had to be. Maybe he was right, and her new mind abilities to interconnect with someone not really there was part of this strange "change" she was undergoing. Maybe Frankie was psychic. All she knew for certain was that she felt strong at this moment. What would happen inside the fortress before her was not quite so certain, however. She opened the car door and stepped out.

Chapter Four

THINGS HAD NOT CHANGED inside the home. They were again ushered to the same room where the will had been read. Rex accompanied her, but then excused himself. She'd not expected that. She'd hoped he would stand at least near, if not beside, her, as she faced…well, whatever it was she was going to face. Looking around the room, she noted that Frankie stood near the wall next to a mirror and a shelf holding the liquid refreshments—of the same strange variety as before. He smiled and gave her a thumbs up. At least *he* was here with her…even though he wasn't really there. A flash in her mind reminded her that Frankie being with her was odd and impossible, but she quickly squashed the thought. Having him there in any form, even her irrational mind, gave her strength—but it sure was crazy.

She took a bottle of water that sat with others in a container of ice, cracked the lid, and took a big swig. It was refreshing and she could feel another kind of strength flow through her veins. Another swig and it felt like she was ready to jump out of her skin, the power was so evident in her body. What was this? Water as an elixir? "Hmmm," she murmured. "I can deal with that." She glanced over to Frankie and he gave her another thumbs-up and then put his index finger to his lips as if to shush her.

In moments, she heard the side door open and in came four male family members. She'd seen them before, young men, interested in her, but too quiet—or scared, or unwilling—to approach her. They merely nodded without smiling, and then went to sit on the couches surrounding the fireplace.

Lenora stood right where she was, sipping water and allowing its properties to filter through her body. The sensation was delicious, and she was agitated that it was here in this gloomy mansion that she'd discovered it and not at her own home with Frankie. She glanced at him and he was beaming. He knew. Somehow, he knew she was gaining energy. And as she gained power, the image of him grew in strength. He was now clear and not quite so dreamlike. He was no longer transparent. He stood like a real person—not the mind's creation he'd been. It was like he was truly there. Of course, this was not likely; still, she relished the thought.

Suddenly, and like a slap in the face, her attention was grabbed by Charlotte, who stood directly in front of her nearly within her personal space. *How did she creep up like that?* thought Lenora as she jumped in surprise. She'd not even heard the woman come into the room.

"Are you with us, or in another place?" asked Charlotte, snapping her fingers in front of Lenora's eyes.

It was true. She'd been in another place. A place where Frankie kept her warm of heart and strong of body and mind. A place she wanted to be, rather than this den of strange beings.

"I'm here," she said softly, a cold, flat tone in her voice. She pushed a strand of hair back from her face that had escaped the band at the back of her head. "I've come to ask for your advice regarding the changes I'm going through. As I understand it, in order to receive your help, I need to put the request to you prior to my 25th birthday. So here I am. What are my next steps?"

Charlotte backed away from Lenora, and stared silently at her, seeming to study her discomfort. "You are aware that you're not welcome here." It was a statement and not a question.

Lenora merely nodded, taking her eyes off Charlotte only long enough to glance at Frankie who was a bit closer to her now and not hanging back.

Charlotte glanced in the same direction, obviously curious as to what drew Lenora's attention from her. It was also obvious that she saw nothing.

"Tell me, then," began Charlotte, flipping her long hair back over her shoulder with one hand, "what kind of changes have you noticed? If any."

It was evident to Lenora that she was being mocked. It was as though Charlotte thought she had no value at all. And maybe she didn't to the family, but she did trust Rex, and if he said she needed this grotesque assembly, then she was willing to concede that there might be some help in it. Still, she wished she'd have something really drastically in-her-face to throw at the woman.

Looking directly into Charlotte's eyes—and mentally pulling back with a twinge of fear—she pulled herself to a straight stance. "Mostly it's been an energy field around me, protecting me from varied things...and the ability to see into the past...and maybe people that aren't there exactly."

Charlotte frowned and glanced away and around the room. "Where's Rex?" she demanded.

Suddenly, he was there, and it was Lenora's turn to frown. Where had *he* come from? He was just *there*. From *nowhere*.

"Yes, dear stepmother," he said, a bit of sarcasm and amusement in his tone. "You rang?"

Charlotte whipped around to him, ready to strike, but seemed to think better of it. "Insolent," she whispered to no one in particular. "One day..." she continued, sashaying to stand in front of him, "Well, we very rarely see you step into the light of day with an opinion. So the wayward bastard son has a stake in this one?"

Rex held a smug grin. "Opinion? I *do* have an opinion about all of this. Don't think I don't remember the shameful time I went through at your hand, Charlotte. Why, if it wasn't for dear Dad, well, who knows what would have become of me." He stepped back from her, removing her from his personal space. "And I don't want to see something worse happen to Lenora. She's a good kid and doesn't have anyone but me to stand beside her."

"How gallant." Charlotte's sarcasm brought a murmured laugh from the other men in the room. She smiled at her own arrogance. "Well, regardless, if she's turning and she has an ability, I need to know."

"It won't be in full swing, even if she does have it. And this is supposed to be training, not testing. We should be gentle and slowly acclimate her to—"

"Hello. In the room here," interrupted Lenora, waving her hand. "You people are all out of your minds." She looked at Rex who was grimacing and shaking his head *no* to her in warning.

"What?" she asked. "I don't need to be treated like a child here. I came with good intentions, and I just want to understand what is going on. I don't know anything about the man you say is my father. I had nothing to do with that. I don't understand this family thing, and I certainly don't understand werewolves."

Everyone but Rex laughed.

"Well, aren't you the spiky one," said Charlotte with nearly a snarl hooked to her words.

"Charlotte," began Rex, "don't. Seriously, you have an idea that she can do something helpful to us, so why not welcome her rather than spurn her?"

Charlotte tilted her head, looking closely at Lenora, then back to Rex. "You may have merit in your opinion, *sweet* cat."

Rex frowned.

Lenora frowned. "Cat?"

"I believe Lenora was discussing her ability to see into the past and to put a force field around herself. Smashing abilities, and just the start," he remarked. There was a bit of pride and a bit of mockery in his voice for having the knowledge.

"So, it's true, then?" Charlotte asked, moving back to Lenora and raising her hand to touch her arm.

Lenora tensed, not wanting the woman to touch her—or to be in any close proximity. And then she smiled as she noted that the woman's hand could not touch her skin. There was indeed a thin energy field around her. Charlotte looked back to Lenora's eyes, lightning flashing. Then

Lenora relaxed and Charlotte's hand went through the force field and rested on her wrist.

Lenora was excited. She had controlled the field by just relaxing, and she could put it up at will, it seemed. Now the fight with her ex-boyfriend made sense—well, part of it anyway. He couldn't touch her because she was not allowing it! Just as she had chosen not to allow Charlotte to lay hands on her. It was all about relaxing the energy.

She watched the woman step back, release her arm, and study her. She was thinking hard, it appeared.

"It never ceases to amaze, these powers that spring forth in you bastards." A growl came from her throat as she moved to the credenza holding the liquid refreshment. She poured herself some of the purple liquid and then stood with her back to the room, sipping. Finally, to Rex, she said, "These unusual powers, Rex...how do you see them developing?"

Rex cleared his throat. "I'm not certain. Lenora is certainly different than any of the others. I've seen no shapeshifting indications. Rather, she is incredibly... aware."

"Aware...." Charlotte turned back to Lenora. "And just what are you aware of?"

Lenora shrugged and stole a glance at Rex. What the hell was he thinking? "I don't really know; things are just starting to...happen. I was able to keep myself from being beaten up by someone, without even knowing how, and I've seen a scene from the past, just like it was a movie." She didn't go further to let Charlotte know she'd seen Frankie in the past because she wasn't sure this made any sense.

Rex added, "She's also seeing ghosts."

"What?" snapped Charlotte, her eyes going wide. "Ghosts?"

Lenora's eyes went wide as well, noticing that Charlotte trembled a bit. Was the woman afraid of ghosts? Of course, it may stand to reason because no matter how scary her wolf persona was, ghosts would be beyond her scope of control. A ghost would not be afraid of anything on this plane.... *Well,* she thought with a bit more confidence flowing into her mind, *this whole family business might not be so bad. If one considered that wolves are in charge.* She shook her head in disbelief even at her own thinking. A month ago, her most abstract thinking had been on canvas.

Charlotte was pacing quietly, and she made eye contact with the other family members in the room, including Rex, who was obviously trying to hide his amusement. She turned back to Lenora, a decision made. "I have decided that we will assist you with your becoming. Rex will be assigned to you, and you are to both report your progress and receive family help via his requests. I would not welcome personal interaction, but will offer any advice needed via Rex." She paused.

Rex took his opportunity to speak. "I'm in agreement that we should help Lenora. It might be that she might sense something upstairs," he said, pulling Charlotte's attention back to him. "And I know it's important, but we should be a bit more tolerant and nurture, rather than attack."

Lenora spoke out. "*She,*" she said with emphasis meaning herself, "should be *educated* and not *delegated.*"

Smirks could be heard from the other young men, but they added nothing more to the conversation.

It seemed that Charlotte was considering her options, hating her on one hand for personal reasons she had no control over, but needing her on the other for whatever was happening in her house. *What the hell's upstairs?* Lenora wondered. It must be bad if Charlotte was wavering in her intolerance of her.

"What's upstairs?" she asked quietly, directing her question to Charlotte.

Charlotte brushed her long hair from her face again. "Frankly, we don't know. We can't see it, but all of us can feel it. Whatever it is should not be in our house."

"What makes you think I can do anything about it? So, now I'm here to be a ghost hunter?" To herself: *Margo's going to get a hoot out of this. But then, I really can't tell Margo about this; she would be in danger. I'll just have to use the skills she's shown me. I can do this,* her mind said, then added, *maybe.*

"I will take a look," she offered, deciding she really had no other choice. "But first, could you tell me what's going to happen to me during this three-month period you talk about?"

Charlotte replied, "We don't know."

Lenora glanced at Rex to see his reaction to her statement. He was nodding his head in the affirmative.

"Great," she mumbled.

Charlotte came close to her again, her face directly in front of Lenora's. "I can tell you that this is a clan of shapeshifters of the wolf variety. We are *not* werewolves. Drivel from the movies; it's an insult. We've always been wolves, until your father began dabbling with the gene pool. Most of his 'experiments' have ended up dead because they were not smart. The only one remaining is Rex, and he is hardly a wolf. We don't really know *why* he is, nor do we care *what* he is. He's not a wolf. We're prepared to think the same of you. This new development, however, has made me rethink my priorities."

"How nice, Mommy," said Rex. "Accepted, but not a part *of*. What *I've* always wanted."

Lenora shifted her weight back and forth and found she could not pull her gaze from the woman in front of her no matter how hard she tried. It was as if she was caught in a spider's web. She just listened, wide-eyed.

"There seems to be something in the attic of our home. One day it was just there. From nowhere. The boys," she said, pointing to the young men, "sensed it first."

One of the young men, a handsome fellow with coal black hair and bright blue eyes, left his seat by the fireplace and approached Lenora. "The attic always had a musty smell. We played there as lads. Lots of historic heirlooms, strange mementoes. Then one day last month, we went up there and something else was in the room. Our senses are keen enough to know that whatever it was, it was dangerous to us."

Rex chimed in, "They were all scared, but I wasn't."

Charlotte puffed air out her nose. "Jolly that."

Rex ignored her. "Lenora, that room upstairs has the same feel as your apartment's basement to me, only worse. And also like the air being pulled out of the car today."

Charlotte snapped in surprise, "Air loss? What is this air loss? She has a weapon already?"

"No," said Lenora in angst. "I don't have anything. I don't understand anything. I had no control over that air thing, Rex." Finally, she was able to take her eyes from

Charlotte. *That woman has power. I might not get out of here alive. But I'd do anything to be out of here now. I don't want to do this test!*

Seeming to have made her decision, Charlotte said, "All right. Enough said about the powers for now. We will explore them with you." She put out her hand to Lenora.

Lenora panicked. The woman was offering her hand to shake. She didn't want to touch her. The woman was not a woman, but a werewolf—despite what she said. She'd seen her change and it was a horrible sight. And one she never wanted to see again. Still, she knew that things were changing in her body and that Rex would help her only if the family approved. Charlotte, that is. She reached out and took Charlotte's hand. Neither woman shook hands, rather they stood holding their right hands, each sizing up the other.

Charlotte released Lenora's hand. "Welcome to the family." She said the words with difficulty.

Lenora, still wide-eyed, merely nodded.

"Well!" said Rex. "This calls for a celebration." He headed toward the beverages.

"This is not a celebration," said Charlotte. "We do not celebrate my husband's infidelity. We merely accept his bastard as part of a greater plan. When the call for action is given, the means for that action is delivered."

Lenora said to herself, *What the hell kind of call did I put out to deserve this? Thanks, Mom.*

Frankie's consciousness hovered at the edge of the room taking in all that was said. He wasn't sure whether this was a help to him or a hindrance. He didn't like Charlotte, for he felt her malice and could see that she would turn on his Lenora at any second, given the right stressor. And he didn't like Rex, either. There was a hormone release whenever he was near his Lenora. He found her attractive and moved close at every opportunity. He used his cat to fashion meetings and to send her attention away from his desire of her. No, he didn't like Rex—or his cat. The cat disrupted those in the basement. The cat disrupted Lenora's normally sharp mind. His Lenora was in danger and so was he.

Lenora looked down the hall that would lead her to the attic. *Isn't* this *just like a horror movie? What the* hell *am I thinking, agreeing to this?* But she knew there was no turning back. Whatever this "family" was, horrible or not, it was the only way she was going to learn what was about to happen to her. And if they didn't know what that was, well, at least they had open minds about it. No one else would believe what she'd been going through. Even Margo would have trouble with this one, and Margo had trouble with nothing otherworldly ever. She could hear her now: "Lenora, get a grip. Werewolves? Right."

The hallway before her, and most probably the second staircase and room beyond, did not match the rest of the

Bradley home in feel. The house itself was a two-level structure—with an attic, it seemed. And it was big. Very large rooms, large foyers, large staircase from the first to the second floor off the huge foyer. It was something out of the cinema, for sure. There were very few furnishings spattered about haphazardly, no carpeting, no drapes on the expansive windows looking out to the woods that seemed to lurk on all four sides of the house. She'd not seen beyond the views from the foyer and the large, what she called, fireplace room. This house was stylish, but missing some really important Feng Shui ideals. Her best description would be elegant stark.

Then they'd taken her up the foyer stairs to the second floor, down the balcony hallway overlooking the foyer for several yards on either side to a door at the end of the hall. They all stood before the door, Charlotte in front, Rex and Lenora right behind, and the four young men hanging back. No one talked; no one moved. It was obvious that no one wanted to open the door. There was an energy behind it that was screaming to get out. But to what end, Lenora did not know.

Lenora's new *fight-or-flight* response had kicked in and she glanced around the hallway behind the four men to see if she could see Frankie. He was always in her mind and she had come to realize—within the last couple hours—that he was more than her imagination. She had a connection to him. It was like telepathy. Yes, that was it—she was becoming telepathic. *Nah, that's not it,* she thought in correction.

Frankie was there, though, standing at the top landing of the staircase, watching them from afar. He too apparently didn't particularly want to know what was behind the door. *If Frankie is uncomfortable, well, that's a bad sign.*

It was clear that no one else saw him, because upon seeing her turn to look back, everyone in the little group followed her gaze. They were all frowning and looking to and fro, between her and the empty hallway.

They don't see him. He's all mine. She saw Frankie's tight line of a mouth slip into a wide smile.

He hears my mind! This is proof that he hears me. She stopped herself from moving to another warm place, which always seemed to happen around Frankie. Instead, she spoke out from her mind: *Frankie? Is it safe for me to do this?*

Frankie, his form clad in what seemed a sharply pressed suit of some kind with a lab coat overtop, walked forward toward her. Lights overhead blinked.

Rex whispered, looking at the flashing hall lights on the ceiling, "That can't be good."

"No," said Lenora, "that's not the problem." Then she looked back to the door that would lead to a wooden staircase upward. She already thought she knew what it would look like and that whatever was up those stairs and beyond the attic door at the top would change everything. She reached out, since Charlotte seemed hesitant, to the handle and turned it. The door swung inward into a very small foyer, nearly the size of an eight-by-ten room. The floor was covered in ugly, scuffed, brown linoleum. To the far side, across from her, was another stairway with about fifteen steps upward and then another door. Behind *that* door was the attic.

They all crowded into the little room, and Frankie stood at the entranceway.

Suddenly, they all winced and looked in panic to each other. Charlotte pushed past Lenora, nearly knocking her to the floor, and the four men and Rex hurried behind her out the door they'd just come through.

Rex grabbed Lenora hard by the shoulders and exclaimed directly into her face, "Stay in here! Stay quiet! Do not open this door to look out or come out, no matter what you hear! If someone comes through that door and it's not me, you run up those stairs into the attic! Do you hear me? That might be the only safe place!"

She merely nodded, fear making her stomach turn over. *Not safe. Anyone near that attic room knows it's not a safe place. What is happening now?* Rex ran out the door, slamming it hard behind her, leaving her in the attic foyer with whatever it was just feet away.

She could feel her body armor force field go into place. It enveloped her like a suit, but despite the known protection, she couldn't move. "Frankie?" she whispered. But he was gone. He'd left with the others. She was alone.

Trying to bite down on her fear before it overcame her, Lenora put her ear against the door to the hallway, and then quickly backed away. At first there had been no sounds, but now she could clearly hear a struggle—and not one she wanted to be close to. Snarling and howling was interspersed with the probable breaking of furniture that would occur in a very bad fight scene. There was a terrible altercation going on below on the first floor of the house.

The sounds went on for a time, and then there was silence. She stayed put for the better part of an hour, though it seemed longer. "I can't stay here," she whispered out loud. "Whatever is going on down there, I need to find Rex and get out." She knew this was not a good idea. Rex would not have warned her to stay behind the door if there were no dangers to consider. He'd told her to go to the attic! And everyone was afraid of the attic. How bad could things be to have him send her there? Still, he wasn't coming for her. Didn't that mean he was in trouble? Of course, she didn't need any wolf trouble. She knew what they looked like, thanks to Charlotte.

"Taking a peek can't hurt," she said just above a whisper. "Frankie, where the hell are you?" But he was nowhere to be seen. That couldn't be a good sign either. He'd been with her throughout this ordeal. What could have spooked him—or all the others for that matter?

Slowly, trying not to make a sound, Lenora turned the doorknob and pulled the door inward just enough to stick her face tentatively around the corner. She peered down the empty hall and strained her ears to hear movement of any kind. Carefully, she slipped into the hallway and, on tiptoes, moved to the second floor balcony, again peeking so that she would be undetected.

She saw nothing in the first-floor foyer, but was startled by movement that came from the other side of the long windows placed on either side of the front door. Her heartbeat sped up and she swallowed hard, hardly able to breathe. Beyond the windows in the front yard were the tail ends of wolves chasing another wolf into the wooded area. She recognized the white coat of Charlotte's counterpart identity leading four gray wolves and an orange cat behind a wolf that was totally black in color. In seconds, they were beyond her sight.

"Wow," she said out loud. "Am I ever stupid. Rex is the cat." There was no Rex the man and Rex the cat. They were one and the same. She couldn't think of that now, however. That too held a ticket to Crazytown. She needed to consider her situation. She was in a house with werewolves, a were-cat (she shook her head at that strange thought), no car to get away, Frankie was gone.... What else could go wrong? *No,* she thought, *don't ever ask that. Never think what else could go wrong? Because something always will.*

It was then she heard the low snarl. While she'd been looking out the front windows, a shiny black wolf had crept out into the hallway from one of the other rooms. It was crouched and ready to pounce. *Do wolves pounce?* she thought absently.

With wide eyes, she pulled at her cross necklace and held it out facing the wolf. "Go away," she said, her voice commanding. "With the power of Christ, I compel you!"

The wolf suddenly metamorphosed into a naked man. And he was rolling on the floor laughing at her. "That's demons, you ninny!" he said, continuing to laugh, but bringing himself to full height in front of her.

Lenora, heart racing and fear grasping her heart like a vice, retorted, "Well, you're a demon, pal. Trust me on that. Stay away!" She still held the cross in front of her.

They studied each other. The "thing" in front of her was amply built and his body was in full response. She tried not to look "there." He had black hair and black eyes—it truly did bring to mind the demons she'd read about and seen on television. Tall, at about six feet, he was a beautiful specimen of male. Male-what she didn't know. Well, yes, she did. Werewolf. Another friggin' werewolf.

"And what do we have here?" he asked. "A pet for Charlotte?"

Less intimidated by the man in front of her, but still knowing he could slam her to the ground in a hot second, she snapped back, "I'm no one's pet. I'm a guest here, and I'll be on my way." She started to step to the right for a path around him. *Of course, this won't work.*

"I don't think so," said the man. "I do believe I have a hostage." He moved forward and grabbed her by the arm.

"*Ow*! That hurts! Get off me, you werewolf!"

He started to laugh again. "Not even afraid of a wolf! Spunk. No matter. If you're here in Charlotte's lair, and you didn't join in the fight, you have other value." He easily dragged her along the hall, though she fought every step.

She could tell he was becoming agitated at her struggle, and she knew that pretty soon, he'd hurt her, maybe kill her. Even so, she fought harder. Why wasn't her armor working? Then she realized. He wasn't trying to hit her or physically attack. Somehow she knew that was not his intent. He was merely pulling her, and that action went right through her force shield. It didn't help that her fear kept her from consciously willing that the armor protect her from him, like it had with Charlotte. She'd been more angry than fearful, if truth be told. Anger controlled, while fear made her powers mush. And that fear would not be going away anytime soon—she couldn't get the vision of the black wolf from her mind. It held her in terror just as Charlotte had that first day.

His hand came up suddenly and boxed her hard on the head. The hallway went black as her struggle stopped and she sank to the floor. *I really need to get control of this power if it's going to be any help to me,* she thought just before the lights went out.

Chapter Five

LENORA AWOKE IN FRANKIE'S ARMS. He held her close and was kissing her forehead as one hand slowly caressed her arm. "Everything will be okay, Doll. You're going to be okay."

At first, his voice and words were calming. Somehow she'd made the jump from attraction to something more when it came to Frankie. It was as though his persona had taken refuge within her heart, and he'd become the most important man in the world. It felt as though she'd already known him for a very long time. She smiled to herself recognizing the rose-colored feelings of love, even if it made no sense at all.

But then other sensations began to kick in. He felt solid to her, yet somehow he also felt like pure energy without a form. She was cold in places where his body did not snuggle next to hers. The lighting was dim and the smell was old and musky. And wet dog odors seemed to permeate her to the core. She remembered, and her body went tense. Looking around, she could see that they were in a large metal-wire cage in what appeared to be a basement with stone walls and cracking mortar. Looking out from behind the bars, she saw two huge dogs—no, wolves—sleeping on the floor.

She whispered, "Frankie, where are we?"

He squeezed her. "I'm not sure. Not too very far from the other wolf house, but they don't know where we are. They just know that you've been taken by this upstart clan of demons."

"Yeah," said Lenora slowly. "Demons. That's right."

"Be very quiet. In fact, just think to me and don't talk. They will hear you, and then the trouble will begin."

Lenora was already tense, but grew more rigid by the moment as she remembered what had happened and now heard Frankie's warning. In her mind she said to him, *What kind of trouble? What are they going to do to us?*

Frankie's mind voice was consoling. *Don't worry, I'll think of something, my lovely Doll. I won't let them vandalize you.*

Vandalize me? What does that mean? Kill me? she thought back quickly.

No, worse. I will not let them mate with you.

What? her mind screamed, *Oh, hell no. We've got to get out of here. And why would they want to mate with me? I'm not their kind!*

Exactly. Frankie's thought paused. *They don't know why you are important to the Bradley family, but they know that if you were in Charlotte's home, you have value.*

Though not speaking out loud, Lenora was nodding in agreement. *That one who got me talked about me having value. But I don't have any value. I mean not their kind of value—whatever that might be....*

Well, despite that, we need to get out of here, he answered.

A voice interrupted. It was the naked man, only now he was wearing clothing. His jeans were tight and muscles rippled through his t-shirt. He was a cliché.

"So you're awake." It was a statement and he didn't expect an answer.

Lenora glanced at Frankie as they sat on the floor of the cage, and Frankie put his index finger to his lips. In her mind she heard him say, *Don't let them know about me.* She nodded.

"I apologize for hitting you, and for the scant accommodations, but we don't know what your powers are. Protection, you see, from a new Bradley."

Lenora remained quiet. Not for effect, though that was obviously what the man in front of her saw, but because she didn't know what to say. Powers. She had a force field. That was it. What good would that do anyone but her—and to be exacting, even she didn't seem to benefit from it much since she didn't know how to totally control it.

"Let me start by introducing myself. I am Divine. And I welcome you to our clan."

Divine? There was nothing divine about this horror of nature.

"Nothing to say?" he asked and smiled. "Come now. What is your name, pretty one?"

She thought quickly about her plight and decided that being accommodating might get her and Frankie out of the cage, but looking to her left, where Frankie had been sitting and holding her, she noted that he was gone. *Great.*

"I'm Lenora, and I don't know anything about anything. Those other people kidnapped me." She paused, then added, "Then you kidnapped me from them. I'd like to know why I'm so important all of a sudden."

Divine paced back and forth in front of the cage, considering what Lenora had said. "I suppose it's not above Charlotte to kidnap someone, but what would be the purpose? She does nothing without purpose."

Lenora merely shrugged and then stood. Though the cage was large, it was not tall, and she had to bend over not to hit her head on the wire above her. What could she say to answer this creature? Just stay on his good side—*if there is one.*

"I don't know, but she is one mean lady and I don't want to be in her clutches again. I just want to go home." What she said was mostly true, so her white lie about not knowing what Charlotte was after went undetected. She sounded like she was telling the truth.

"It's also not beyond Charlotte to steal someone away to offer as a celebratory dinner." He stopped pacing and looked closely for her reaction.

It didn't take long, because what he said rang true. "Holy—they were going to *eat* me? Oh, this day cannot get worse." *Hell, I jinxed myself again!*

Lenora moved right up to the bars in front of Divine; it was difficult to bite the fear, but she managed. Her words and very demeanor were of paramount importance right now. It would mean the difference between being caged like an animal or loose. She needed to tread carefully.

"Could you let me out of here? I certainly pose no threat—you already know that." Would girly eyes work on a wolf?

Divine laughed. "So dramatic, pretty one. I can let you out, because I know you know that you could be wolf meat in a matter of seconds should you step the wrong way." With that, he glanced back to the other wolf lying on the floor. This one turned into a man immediately in the same fashion as Charlotte had with a spinning circle thing.

She'd never get used to that. It was like a whirlwind of dust or mist or air of some kind that moved in tornado fashion around the animal, nearly hiding the creature inside it. Then out stepped a naked human. This new wolfman moved to a wall where a key was held on a hook—*very pirate like*, she thought. The cage was unlocked and she was able to move out and stand straight. As she did, she brushed against the man freeing her. His male appendage shot out, large and angry.

Lenora swallowed hard.

"Stand down, Friar," said Divine and then to her, "You'll have to forgive our small pack. There are no females and we've all longed for that kind of companionship."

Lenora now blinked. Join them? Oh no. This was not happening.

"But I'm not like you. I'm not a werewolf. That wouldn't work at all," she said, looking at Friar wolf narrowly.

"We are not werewolves, dear Lenora. We are a wolf clan, here for over 400 years. We were the largest in the territory, including the Bradley clan, but we've lost most to attrition. As far as we know, there are no other female wolves in our part of the clan. Eventually, we will be forced to take human women to continue our line. They will not be full bred, but will still carry our genes forward at least. The outcomes will be strange and varied.... Ah! Now I know why you are mingling with the Bradleys. The elder for many years has been experimenting with ways to continue our species and has created many a hybrid. Is that what you are, Lenora?"

Hells bells. Now what? Frankie, where the hell *are you?*

Suddenly, Frankie was there right next to the large picture window over the sink looking into the woods. Did all these wolf clans live in houses in the woods? *Well, of course they do. Where else?*

I'm right here, said Frankie, not even looking at the other wolfmen in the room. *Reconnaissance.*

"Well, it's about time you showed up," said Lenora out loud and with great irritation. She immediately recognized her mistake.

Divine and Friar stopped and looked at her. Divine said, "Who are you talking to?"

Great, they can't see you, Frankie, she said in her mind.

Too late, he returned. *They're onto you.*

Backpedalling, Lenora said, "No one and everyone. I was glad that someone showed up to find me out there. It was about time...."

The men looked back and forth at one another.

"We're wolves, not idiots. Not only are you talking to someone who we can't see, we also know you're checking the place over for escape routes. Wolves know at every moment what their prey is doing."

Lenora thought she'd been discreet about looking around, but obviously not. "Well … of course I was looking around. Wouldn't you after you'd been in a cage? So touchy. And prey? Really? We were getting on so well."

Divine smiled. "No, not prey. You're correct in that. We would never eat one of our own hybrids. That's what you are, Lenora. Isn't that right?"

The Friar spoke up. "What do you think she would have if she mated with one of us? She's already half-blood. That would make an offspring quarter blood."

"Yes," said Divine, "but it would be a quarter blood mine, a quarter blood Bradley. That's got to be good."

"True," replied Friar.

Lenora shook her head. Men were insufferable. "In the room," she said in agitation, her hands planted on her hips. This new development, though scary, at least gave her some power. These wolves needed her to keep their line going. If they were right, Charlotte was the only female around, and she didn't look like she was looking to get pregnant anytime soon. *Not that I want to. The last thing I need is to mate with a wolf. How does that even happen?* "I'm not planning to have a baby wolf anytime soon."

"Well," said Divine, "time will tell. Now. Let's talk about the friend you are talking to."

Frankie! she called out in her mind. *What's going on? Is someone coming to rescue me?* To Divine, "I don't know what you're talking about."

"Your heart rate has doubled and your respiration is fast. We know you're lying. Out with it...unless you'd like to begin the mating process as a starter. It can be quite pleasant, you know. The process happens when we are half human, half wolf. It should be quite exhilarating for you." He nodded to Friar who rose from the kitchen chair and began to turn, only he stopped midway, while he still had a man's erection and lower body. The top half was monstrous—not a full wolf, but rather like the movie monsters' version. Big teeth, yellow eyes, and hair everywhere.

Frankie was in her head. *Tell them. You don't owe the Bradleys any allegiance. Charlotte doesn't even want to come after you. Rex the cat is out in the woods looking, but his skills don't match the wolves. And he's a ways from here. Use this group against the others so you can be safe.*

"Oh, all right," said Lenora to Divine and stepped back from Friar. "Call off your dog."

Divine let out a laugh. "Down, Friar, and put your pants on."

Friar quickly disappeared in a dust cloud and when the dust settled, he was back to a man—still with an erection. "Damn," he said.

"So," encouraged Divine.

"They've got a ghost or something in their attic and they think that it's the end of the world. I apparently can see ghosts. And they think I can get rid of it."

"Hmmm," said Divine. "Not a hybrid then. A human who hunts ghosts. We've seen all the television shows about them."

Lenora couldn't believe her luck. They'd jumped to a conclusion that was incorrect. But it did help her greatly. Even Frankie was smiling.

"Yes, right. That's what I do. And Charlotte seems to think that there is something like that...ghosts...that is, in their attic. And it's a secret. So you can't tell anyone, you know." She glanced at Frankie and he was shaking his head.

"You did better, Lenora, not talking." Divine was frowning. "The truth now. We know about the attic."

Just then, a crash sounded from the front of the house. The men looked at Lenora. She merely shrugged. "Not me; I'm here with you."

"Check it out," Divine ordered Friar. "I smell something, but I'm not exactly sure what it is. It's not wolf, though. It's not the Bradleys." Then he whispered, "Thank goodness."

Friar didn't bother to move now that he was panted and settled at the kitchen table, but glanced up from a newspaper he'd picked up, barely noticing Lenora or Divine. He said, "I saw a cat go by the front window."

Divine and Friar said at once with boredom in their tones, "Rex."

Lenora blinked. Rex? Was he coming to save her? But wait, they were saying "cat." She spoke up, "Rex the cat, or Rex the man?"

"One in the same," came a voice from the kitchen door. There stood Rex the man, brushing off his trousers and smiling widely at Lenora. "Guess you met the rebels of the family here."

Lenora frowned, confused now. "This is family, too? They kidnapped me! Kept me in a cage all night! And that one knocked me out," she said, pointing to Divine.

Rex shook his head and glared at Divine. "You kept her in a cage? And hit her?"

"Well, we didn't know what she was. She coulda turned into a hyena for all we know," defended Divine. "With Charlotte so interested in her, what were we to think?"

Lenora interrupted, "In. The. Room. What were you to think? Well, asking me, for one thing, would have helped. And not kidnapping me, for the next thing!"

Rex said to Divine, "She doesn't understand things yet, dear brother."

The two men said together, "Half-brother."

Friar added, "And tolerant half-brothers we are, putting up with a mangy cat."

"About that," said Lenora.

Rex cut her off. "No time for that now, Lenora." Then to the men, "We've other things to discuss. Charlotte is on the warpath now because you blatantly came in and took her new toy."

"Toy?" said Lenora. She had her hands on her hips again and her mouth was a tight line.

"Not now," said Divine, then to Rex, "We had to take her. If she'd gone up into that attic...well, we all have to be prepared. Who knows what's up there or why?"

"Did you show her the trap?" inquired Rex.

"No," replied Divine. "She's ..."

"Yes, I know. A handful."

They nodded in agreement, then looked at Lenora.

"You bet I'm a handful, and what do you expect? I'm living my life—happily, I might add—and painting my canvases and generally moving right along." Lenora waved her hand to show movement. "Then, *all of a sudden*, I'm a freak in a werewolf sideshow, seeing things from the past, sporting armor, and keeping time with a cat...." She paused and said in question, "... that's a human?"

They all just nodded.

Then Rex yawned and said, "Sorry about that."

Friar added, "Now that we know who you are...it's your mother's fault. She should have told you. She knew. And we all knew her, but she hightailed out of our lives and swore you wouldn't have to grow up like we did."

Divine whispered to no one in particular, "Great lot of good that thinking did."

Lenora was still in a cloud of uncertainty and a storm cloud of angry. "Kidnapped. You kidnapped me under the most frightening circumstances. A wolf staring me down until I ... what? Fainted? And you hit me? Or did you do some other horrendous thing to me?"

"You fainted after I tapped you on the head," said Divine. "I would never have drugged you."

"And how am I supposed to know what you would and wouldn't do?" She looked around the room at each of them and then said, "I'm going home."

Divine spoke up. "Well, no. No, you're not. We need you here. Rex has predicted you to us and we need your help."

"Everyone needs my help. What the hell? I'm a painter. I sell frames. I don't have a clue about ghosts and werewolves."

Again, the men exchanged glances. Rex said, "I've not been entirely forthcoming with you, Lenora. At first I thought you were just like me—the old man's bastard. But in a short time, I began seeing that you were much more than me. And when I found that you were able to see things that were not there, well, we have a problem that needs investigating."

Still worried about her surroundings and her decision to follow the advice of Rex, who was certainly not human in the real sense of what humanity was, Lenora remained quiet, searching inside herself for an answer—a voice, perhaps, that would give her good counsel. And speaking of counsel, where had Frankie gotten to?

I'm right here, Frankie said, popping up in her mind's eye. *I'm afraid I don't know what to advise you to do. I don't know what these creatures have in mind for you. I do know that you will be getting stronger—it's only a matter of time. Your energy is explosive.*

In her mind she answered, *Yeah, but will there be enough time to get me out of this mess? They were going to feed me to whatever was in the attic.*

No, I don't think so, Frankie responded. *They are frightened and are looking for someone to provide explanations so a plan can be forged. They are in attack mode, yes, but you are not their prey.*

Not now, maybe, she said. Looking up, she noted that all three men were looking at her oddly. They seemed to be small dogs tilting their heads to the side when there was a question with something inserted that they recognized.

"She's talking to someone," said Friar.

Lenora started as she realized they had a bit of telepathy themselves. They'd had to, though. Wolves running wild must have a way to communicate beyond the normal variety of beast. They were wolves, but more, weren't they?

"It's probably that blasted Frankie," snapped Rex. "I sure wish you'd tell me, Lenora, who that guy is. I've yet to sense him and yet he seems to be floating around in your head nonstop."

Lenora snapped back from her internal dialog with Frankie. "I just want to go home, Rex. You promised you'd stand by me—or at least that's the impression I'd gotten. But you, as it were, threw me to the dogs." She looked around her. "Where's my purse? You have it, I saw it. I'm leaving." Then directly to Rex, "Even if I have to walk."

"You won't have to walk, but please, let's talk about this," Rex said moving forward to put his arm around her shoulders.

She shrugged it off. "Enough talk. I—"

Divine broke in. "I'm sorry, but there's not going to be any leaving. Lenora, I recognize your place in the family. I do. So does Friar. So do the cubs back at Charlotte's," he began. "But you can't go anyplace until you see my room."

"And just what does that mean?" Her words rose an octave with anger. "See your room. Am I now to be mated with you...you...things as well?

Friar answered, "Now that hurts."

Rex waved them all away. "Okay, there's not meant to be any intrigue here for any of this. The facts are as Charlotte stated before. We don't know what's in the attic. And we don't know what's in Divine's room, either. We do know that Charlotte does not know that Divine has a room in this sub house as she does in her attic. That would really set off her panic button, and trust me when I say: No one wants a panicked Charlotte."

Suddenly, Frankie was there in the room; at least she could see him, although the others apparently still could not. She thought to him, *What should I do? I don't mind telling you that I'm scared of these guys. Well, except Rex, though I should be afraid of him as well. It's just that he's a cat and not a wolf. Listen to me, will you. Shapeshifters and I'm standing here deciding whether one is—*

Stop, came Frankie's voice in her mind. *Your fear is making you ramble. I don't believe these men are your enemies; rather, they are here to help you do what you were meant to do.*

You believe that, she said, watching him as he sauntered around the room. Then she coughed as she noticed the others were watching her watch nothing move around the room.

Friar said, "I don't know about any of you, but I think she's crazy. Who's she talking to?"

Lenora's gaze went directly to Friar's. How did he know she was talking to someone?

He said, "Just a skill I have. I can't make out everything, just a little, but I know a conversation when I hear one."

Rex interrupted, "Frankie again, right?"

Lenora nodded.

"So he's a ghost?" continued Rex. "Does he have a role to play in this?"

Lenora shook her head. "No, he's not a ghost, just a friend I can converse with in my head." She frowned. It sounded odd, even to her.

Friar said, "He's a ghost all right. Well, sort of...."

Divine stepped closer to Lenora and surveyed her with narrowed eyes, but he spoke to the others. "Not a ghost, eh? Well, I'm not so sure. That's what Charlotte thinks this is. Ghosts taking over the pack." He laughed. "She's got it wrong, as always." Then to Lenora, "So what's the deal, ghosty girl?"

Lenora stepped away from him and closer to Rex. "Haven't a clue."

"What's your friend say?" asked Divine.

"He's okay with us," said Friar. "I did get that. I think she's gonna help us. She believes in Rex, anyway."

Rex smiled and mouthed, "Thank you."

Lenora rolled her eyes. "This sucks. Kidnapped by werewolves, ghost rooms, and dogs eavesdropping on my thoughts."

"And love for a...whatever this thing is you're conversing with," said Friar.

"He's not a thing, I told you," said Lenora, "and how do you know how I feel about him or anything anyway?" She tossed her head. "You don't, that's how."

Divine moved toward the side door off the kitchen that led down a darkened hallway. "Enough of this. We all here have separate powers and abilities. That's no secret. And we all have a similar goal—to find out what's in these ghost rooms."

Lenora whispered, "I don't."

"Remember," said Divine, "you're dealing with wolves and a cat. Our hearing is beyond anything you could possibly imagine. You won't be able to sigh without our hearing it." He went silent for that to sink in and then added, "You may not see the importance now, but soon you will be as much a part of this intrigue as any of us. Especially since you're the one who has been sent to deal with it."

"Sent by who?" Lenora asked, a haughtiness to her voice that seemed to boom across the small kitchen space.

No one spoke. It was obvious to her that no one knew. Still, here she was. And Frankie had said they were okay.

"Well, I still don't know why you had to storm Charlotte's house and scare the friggin' life out of me. Then whisk me away to this place."

"Our home for now," said Friar. "Until Charlotte is put in her place. Or until she learns that we're not a part of her problems, but part of her solutions."

"Fine," said Lenora. "Where's this ghost room?"

Divine, with one hand, waved her toward the dark hallway. "Last door on the left."

"Sounds like a horror movie," Lenora whispered, and slowly stepped forward into the hall.

The room was before all of them now, and the men were obviously feeling nothing in comparison to Lenora's shattering mind. She looked at the door, and though she knew it was not moving in the physical sense, she could feel the wood of the door throbbing, its material properties shifting and rippling as if it were alive with millions of insects writhing on it. But as she reached out to touch it, there was no movement. Still, the feel of a drumming behind it was unmistakable. There was something huge behind this door. She'd not been this close to Charlotte's attic entrance, but this one, standing in front of it, touching it, gave her the feeling of a great power beyond. Something, that if not handled properly, could be not only her undoing but also the end of all things. Lenora tightened her muscles. How could she sense this? Where had all these abilities come from? These entities around her, the wolves and a cat, Frankie. Where had they come from? None of these people had been anywhere within her boring life before. Yes, now it all seemed boring, though prior she'd gone through life as a happy and adventurous person. That was nothing now. This was reality, and more of it stood right behind the door, as well. A new reality, of that she was sure. There would be no turning back if she opened this doorway—for yes, it was a doorway, a path, an entrance to something no one could comprehend as she could.

Lenora swallowed hard, looked back at the men and cat (for Rex had turned animal) behind her. "Now or never," she whispered, and they all nodded.

Lenora opened the door, allowing it to swing inward easily. Everyone held their breaths.

"Nothing," said Divine. "All this intrigue for nothing."

But Lenora's eyes were wide. Nothing? They saw nothing? Inside the room she could see a green swirling ...tornado. It swirled in a stable manner, a whirring sound loud and monotonous in her mind. The sound was deafening, and it pushed inside her brain in a fashion that tempted her to stop thinking, to succumb to a power she could not explain. It took all she could manage to turn back to Divine who was right at her elbow now, his hand gripping her upper arm.

"You can't see it?" she asked in a loud voice. She was trying to call out to him over the drumming sound.

"See what? There's nothing there. Why are you yelling?"

Suddenly, Rex jumped into her arms, the fur on his back standing straight up. She knew he could see what she was seeing, and for some reason, she knew it had to do with his power to change into something other than the human.

"You have to change to see it," she called out. "I don't know how I know, but I know.'

Behind her, Divine let go of her arm and turned to Friar. "You heard the lady."

Lenora turned again to the energy in the room and didn't even look back to see what she knew would frighten her from behind. Werewolves were ultimately more frightening physically, but this tornado in front of her was more powerful and there for a reason. She now could feel Divine's wolf snout at her leg and she felt the cat's claws at her chest. Slowly she reached out to touch the swirling green body of energy before her. Her hand made contact.

In seconds, she was sucked into the tornado and was swirling upward into an even bigger mass that was above the house moving skyward. It was as though she'd gone right through the roof, solid as it was. Rex was still in her arms and she was squeezing him. He howled like no cat should.

Trying to look down as she turned, she caught sight of two werewolves swirling in the same energy, the green churning nearly stealing away their images. She could see terror on their wolf faces and knew that her own held that same anguish. They were all in the energy, passing up and through the clouds into a black, star-filled mass. Suddenly, she felt the sharp jarring of hitting the ground. Instinctively, she rolled in such a way not to squash the cat and, as she touched ground, let him go. The tornado energy seemed to wink out of existence.

Seconds later, one by one, two wolves seemed to fall from the sky in the same manner that she and Rex had. One minute not there, the next in full animal form beside her. The animals were quickly on their feet, fully alert, growling, and in attack mode. She stood up from her fallen status and stared at them. The wolves were no longer a fear for her, for this energy field went well beyond any known dread she'd ever experienced. The wolves, in a sense, were just like her, searching for something that explained what was happening to them. Even seeing Charlotte for the first time did not compare to this experience inside the energy.

The wolves and cat before her were all poised to attack, but they were not looking at her. Rather they stared beyond her. Lenora turned to see what was scaring them.

She pulled in her breath and a whimper came out of her mouth as she saw what the animals were looking at. It was Frankie. It was the scene she'd seen in her bedroom that night. It was a time past. Frankie was with the man at the old box-like machine, just as she'd seen him before. And as before, he turned to look at her, but this time, the scene did not disappear.

"Thank God you're here, Lenora," Frankie said. "We're running out of time!"

Lenora stood stunned.

Frankie looked behind her to the cat and two wolves. "You brought them." He did not sound pleased. "Can they change so that they don't scare anyone?"

She glanced back at the men and nodded. It was as if she were in charge; she felt empowered and was able to give the order without flinching. Turning back to Frankie, she could hear the rustle of change behind her. "Frankie…"

"Yes, it's me. I'm sorry you had to find out this way, but once I saw you before, I knew this was to be your entranceway."

"Before…" she began. "Before when I saw this very scene, you were waiting for me to come here then. But I'd seen you before that…at my shop…in the park…my apartment…. Everywhere."

Frankie moved across the room, for now there was no sign of the green energy. There were only four walls and a scantly furnished office. "*Before* for *you*, was just *seconds before* for me. I can't explain it, but there's some kind of energy force field here that moves through the multiverse. I was just getting used to it. And no one believes me except my associate here and, well, we're the only ones who really saw it."

The man using the computer-like machine stopped his clicking and looked up at them. He waved, frowned, and then went back to this work.

"But I saw you in my time with me." Her statement was flat. *Strange that I'm able to accept all this without judgment. Wolves, cats, energy fields, time travel, multiverses…ghosts.*

Rex stepped up. "So, this whole thing in the two rooms back where we came from leads to here. Wherever here is." He was still poised for quick action, even outside his cat demeanor.

Lenora started in surprise. All three men were changed, to be sure, but they stood in tattered piles of clothing—all except Rex. It made sense, though. How else would they be? Clothing would be a problem going back and forth between animal and human. She'd not noticed that with Charlotte—the pile of clothes, that is—but she'd been too frightened to look behind the gruesome spectacle before her at that time.

Frankie frowned. "You and...those things...shouldn't be here," he said to Rex, his mouth crinkled into distaste. "Lenora is to save us. You will only be in the way."

Divine now spoke. "Don't know who you are, nor do we care. But whatever that mass is in our house is a danger that shouldn't be there. And it obviously has to do with something here." He looked at Lenora. "This is the ghost you've been dealing with?"

"Uhmm, well, I...I didn't think Frankie was a ghost...." She looked to Frankie for explanation.

Frankie, too, was uncertain of his words, but he moved forward and took Lenora's hand. "In truth, Doll—I mean Lenora—I don't know much about any of this, but a magnetic field of some kind came into being when I was working on a thesis plan for what you call an electromagnetic vapor attractor."

Lenora and the three men stood silent with looks of confusion on their faces.

"What?" Lenora simply said.

Before more could be said, a commotion could be heard out in the hall beyond the room where they stood. A woman was yelling, "Just get the holy creation out of my way, or I'll knock you down. And don't think I can't. Or won't with the least provocation."

A male voice said, "No, ma'am, I'm sure you can do all you say, but it's my job to tell you that it's classified in there. No exceptions."

"I know that; I've got clearance. It's me who put the security in place, moron."

"Well, I don't think so, ma'am," said the man.

"Chauvinistic, piece of rat meat, get...out...of... my... way! Last chance."

Frankie jumped in obvious distress. "Quick! Hide behind those cabinets!" he said, moving to the door and grabbing the handle. "And don't come out no matter what!"

Lenora, Rex, Divine, and Friar glanced at each other and shuffled back to the cabinets.

"Quick, I said," ordered Frankie. Once they were behind the cabinets, he casually opened the door. "Hello, Doll."

Lenora peeked around the edge of the cabinet and saw that a woman had walked into the room, dressed in a business suit with heels to match, though they were blocky and ugly. This was a woman of straight lines. She held herself erect and walked in a manner that shouted "in charge." The woman's back to the cabinets, all Lenora could see was blondish hair pulled up high and secured in a bun at the back of her head. And that Frankie was intimidated by her.

The woman said, "I can't get by the security in front of the container room now. I don't think they're on to me, but still...something's going on." She began to pace.

It was then that Lenora saw her face. She sucked in her breath and backed up against Friar with a jerk. Turning to him, her eyes were wide. All the naked men and Rex mouthed at the same time, "What?"

Lenora just shook her head and flattened herself against the nearby wall. Her face was ashen.

Rex and Divine snuck a look around the cabinet's edge and both came back as quickly as Lenora did.

"What?" mouthed Friar, his hand up in agitated confusion.

Divine grabbed him and gave him a small push to the side of the cabinet.

When he turned back to them after looking around it, he pointed to Lenora and mouthed, "It's *her*!"

They all stood stunned. Lenora, worse for the wear, her hands shaking, eyes wide, was showing signs of shock. There was a second Lenora.

Chapter Six

FRANKIE AND THE SECOND LENORA were still **talking** about an electrical experiment of some kind and a disappearance of people on their team.

A tad calmer now, noting it was unlikely the woman would discover them, Lenora forced herself to breathe slowly, to listen to what they were saying, and to think. *I watch too much television and read too many books,* she thought, remembering science fiction novels and movies where there were doppelgangers or time travel instances where meeting yourself was a really bad thing for a timeline. So where *were* they and what *was* this timeline? What had made the green tornado she'd just been exposed to? How had it transported them?

She looked at the three men, who'd taken to shivering—it was cold in this office-like space. She could see folded blankets in a far corner, but she wouldn't be able to get to them without being seen or heard. They would just have to wait until the woman left.

The group stood quietly and listened to Frankie and the woman talking, but the more they heard, the more confused they became.

"I don't know what to do about reporting them missing," Frankie was saying to the woman. "Lenora, I think they went through that electromagnetic force field into that other time—that other place."

Lenora? thought Lenora. *He called her Lenora.* That *did* make sense, since she obviously looked exactly like her, and maybe that meant she *was* her. Now *that* didn't make sense. And who were these other people he was talking about? Was the force field the entrance into the room at Divine's place and also into the attic where Charlotte lived?

Lenora watched Rex motion to Frankie to speed it up, but Frankie only shook his head in annoyance.

"What?" said the woman appearing to be Lenora. "You look annoyed. And that is *not* my fault. If you'd been at the controls, you'd have seen them disappear and maybe could have prevented it. Now, not only do we have to find them, we have to make sure we don't get killed, or worse, doing it."

"I know, Doll," said Frankie. He fought a yawn, but it slipped out anyway.

"Keeping you up, am I? Do I need to find someone else who understands the importance of all this? And *Franklin,* if you call me Doll one more time, I'm going to find a doll and shove it up your—"

"No need," answered Frankie, holding up his hands. "Just my habit of endearment and you know that, too." He glanced at the group peeking from behind the cabinet and smiled slightly so that the hiding Lenora could see.

"Keep your endearment, and find out where our people have gone." Then to the machine operator, "Davis, come along with me. I have some tasks for you."

The operator looked up from his screen and equipment. "I'm kinda busy here at the moment, ma'am. Someone has to watch out for—"

"It wasn't an invitation. I'm ordering. Now let's go." Her feet were planted firmly on the floor and her hands were on her hips.

The man rose slowly from his chair and shrugged at Frankie. He glanced at the cabinets and nodded to Divine, who was in eye view of the man. Then he followed the not-so-nice Lenora out of the room. The door slammed behind them.

Once the woman who was Lenora in this strange place was gone, the "real" Lenora stepped from behind the cabinets, moved to the corner of the room, grabbed the blankets and threw them toward the men.

"I know you have questions," began Frankie.

"Ya think?" snapped Lenora. "What's going on, Frankie? What year is this? I thought you were a dream in this place, and if you're real here, who is the Frankie I've been seeing back where we came from?"

Friar, wrapped in an army blanket, spoke up. "The one back there isn't real. He's a ghost. You see him, and no one else does. And you're in 1944. See that newspaper on the table?"

"1944. Great. There's a year I never wanted to visit. Oh, and that's right about us not seeing you," said Rex.

"No," replied Lenora, "that's not right. People see him...and he and I have a special connection." Then, pointing to the present Frankie, "Not like with him, who I haven't a clue who he is or what we're doing here. Or how we got here. And who that woman is who seems to be me but can't be."

"We came through the portal," said Divine. "I'm stating the obvious, of course. But I believe that in both our house and Charlotte's, there is a portal to this time and place."

"Yes, to the portal," said Frankie. "I don't know exactly how it works, but it seems to be tied to some research I've been doing in regards to our experiments with medical manipulation with DNA via electromagnetic attraction to fight disease."

Lenora and the men just looked at him with stone faces. "And..." prompted Rex.

Frankie shrugged. "All I know is that if my Lenora here should meet all of you...well, I don't think that's good."

"Disturbs the space time continuum?" said Lenora. There was sarcasm in her tone.

It was now Frankie's turn to show a blank face. "I don't understand what you just said."

"How about your man, Davis? He saw us," said Divine.

"He's okay," Frankie said. "He's my assistant and has been through quite a bit with me these last months. It seems that about a month ago, though, things began changing and I began to see, what I'm thinking now, is your world." Then, nodding to Lenora, "And you."

"I've been seeing you, as well," she stated.

"Melodramatic," offered Rex. "Things are a bit clearer now as far as what your abilities will become in...what, two months' time now? You see the past and can travel to it via these portals. You have a protective shield. And you are related to the family via these more subtle physical changes, rather than being full-blown shapeshifters as we are."

Lenora had remained quiet through this discussion, her heart aching without knowing why. Frankie, the one she knew from *her* side, was a shadow of the person from this time, who was a part of another woman's life. He had referred to her as "my Lenora" and the tone he used was a warmer sort than the rest of his words. He would not be *hers*. She frowned. It wasn't as if this line of thinking had even occurred to her, but if she were honest, she had to admit she had been leaning that way. She longed for him and looked for him at every turn. With all the changes around her, he was the only thing that felt safe. And safe—above everything else—was something she craved and positively needed at this time.

But it wasn't just that. There was the matter of the twirling tendrils making love to her. That, somehow, had been Frankie. Maybe not the physical man, but his thoughts, his will, his desire that had entered her in the most personal way possible. Could she ever get that from her mind? Wouldn't that then be the bar from which she judged every man for the rest of her life? That was a resounding yes.

"You're too quiet," Rex said, now very near at her elbow. He touched her arm gently. "I know that a lot has happened and that most women would have crumbled into a lunatic state by now, but you're stronger than that, love. You've got Bradley blood in your veins."

That snapped her to. "Bradley blood? Thanks for the friggin' reminder. It brings to mind that not only don't I understand any of the crap related to *that*, I don't understand why we're here either." She moved away from Rex to stand in front of Frankie. "And you. What the hell were you doing, coming into my world and turning my life upside down? What was your game?"

Frankie took a step back. "No game, Doll," he answered, reaching his hand out to her.

Lenora took a step backward then, too. "Do. Not. Call. Me. Doll."

"Sorry. The problem is that our people are missing. Well, we actually think we know where they are now. Rather, *I* think *I* know. I haven't told anyone yet. I don't think we can get to them without causing a great deal of trouble. As I was trying to figure that out, Davis stumbled on a strange frequency while using the new coding lines. It opened the new portal near your quaint little shop. It was my idea to go through to your time and retrieve our people and then come right back here."

Everyone was frowning now, and they all looked at each other in disbelief.

"They definitely don't have television in this time," said Lenora. "Otherwise, he'd know how stupid that idea was. I mean *is*."

Divine broke in. "First things first. We need clothing so we can move about in a fashion that won't land us in more trouble than we're already in. We're quite conspicuous."

"Yes," agreed Frankie, "that does seem like appropriate thinking. I can take care of that. Stay hidden and I'll be right back." He glanced at each man, apparently estimating their sizes, and then left through the only door in the room.

Once he was gone, Rex turned to Lenora. "Okay, *Doll*. So what's next? How do we get out of this place? This is nostalgic to be sure, but I don't think any of us really fit in here." Looking at the diplomas mounted on the wall in ornate frames, he added, "This is obviously a research university. Possibly out of our league," he said to his counterparts.

"Tell me about it," said Lenora in a whisper, and then louder, "and don't call me, *Doll*. Seriously now, remember me? I'm the one needing help with whatever is going to happen to *me* over the next three months before I *really* change, and *you* are supposed to be providing that. Think I know what's going on here? I'm still trying to swallow that you're a cat that has been hanging out at my house spying on me when I sleep and take a shower."

"No," said Friar, "you didn't..."

"That's just wrong," added Divine.

"What?" said Rex. "I wasn't spying; I was just making sure she was all right. I mean she kept talking about this Frankie character, and who knew who or where or what he was? I was making sure she was safe. You know how it goes and how strange creatures with even stranger powers gravitate to us."

"Right," replied Lenora. "Anyway, here nor there. I don't know what's next or anything at all. My thought first is: How do we get back to our time? If I'm creating these portals with my 'change,' I don't know how I'm doing it, or why I'd be doing it."

Divine said, "There's something else important here. There are missing people involved who obviously went through the portal to our time. We need to know more about who *they* were and anything else we can find out. If they show up in Charlotte's attic, or they're already there...well, let's just say that won't be their best day."

The men were all nodding.

"What *is* it with her?" demanded Lenora. "She is a first-class witch," and then she mumbled, "Or worse."

They continued nodding.

"Would she kill them?" she asked.

Still they nodded.

"Well, that just moved to the top of the list as far as I'm concerned," replied Lenora.

It was then that Frankie burst back in through the door, allowing it to slam behind him. He carried a large, tan duffel bag and threw it on the floor in front of the pack. "Here. I hope these things fit. It's the best I could do raiding the locker room in such a quick fashion. There will be students without clothes complaining."

The men moved forward and Rex opened the bag, distributing the clothing. Lenora grabbed Frankie's arm and pulled him to the side a few steps away.

"Tell me more about the people who disappeared. What's that all about? What happened to them?" she asked in a whisper.

"We don't know," Frankie answered. His brow was wrinkled and worry was etched in the lines on his face. "Just like you were *not* here one minute and the next you were, it was the same with them. They were here working right alongside Davis and me ... and then ... they weren't."

Lenora frowned. "Why weren't *you* or Davis taken?"

Frankie shrugged. "I don't know, but then something else peculiar happened. I started having hallucinations and blackouts. Only in this room, though. That's when I'd find myself with you."

"Well, you're right to worry about it, because I haven't a clue what to do next. It could be that this whole thing is related to a change that is supposed to happen to me—and that's a long story. Well, not long and you've heard most of it already, but it could all be me. But it could also be what you people are doing here, too. How could what *you* are doing *here* be connected to what *we* are doing *there*?" She was frowning, and though she was trying to look confident in front of him, she knew that terror had to be evident in her eyes, for this situation, despite her seeming to handle things well, was just a weak front.

"I don't know about any relationship between our times, but there is one consistency," said Frankie. "There are two Lenoras. That has to mean something."

"You're right, of course." she said, thinking out loud. "That is so strange. We're not seeing two of anybody else, only me." She paused. "And I must say, I don't like me very much here."

"Be careful with your words," Frankie said, his tone dropping, "She's *not* you, and I love her."

Lenora struggled not to show surprise or the snap of hurt. She'd adopted the view in the prior days that he was *her* Frankie, and it never occurred to her—well, maybe it had when she'd first seen her doppelganger, but she'd pushed it way far away—that this woman in this place was his paramour, and she was just a lookalike from some strange place. "Then what was all that stuff about in my bedroom?" she asked. Her words were snippy though she was trying not to let anger show in her voice. He'd broken through her defenses and had seduced her in a way that was unconscionable. Hiding it was difficult.

"I don't know what you mean," he said.

The blank look on his face clearly showed this was true. That surprised and worried her. What had that been then? She watched as he turned away from her, running his fingers through his hair (that looked to have too much product in it for her taste).

"Look," he said, without turning around, "something essential is going on here, but I don't understand what it is. It must have to do with you and my Lenora, because you and she are the only real bizarre thing."

"Oh, really? You don't think portals and wolves and cats that turn into people and vice versa are strange?"

"You know what I mean. Something has to do with the two of you." He turned back to her and looked her squarely in the eyes. "But I can't tell her about this. She can't...I mean she *won't* believe it—even if she sees you, she won't believe it. She'd kill you first, thinking you were a spy or something sent by God or some government to foil our efforts. It's all about her work. Her work her work her work ..."

"Just what *is* her work?" Lenora said in barely more than a whisper.

Frankie turned back to her with a blank stare. "It's top secret."

"Oh, great. Like I'm going to tell anyone who it will matter to in my time."

"It just might, but I do see your point," he said.

Still, he was hedging. She could tell he was uncertain trusting her, and that hurt. He knew she needed to know, but he also knew that if the Lenora in this time found out he'd told her … well, he'd be in some kind of hot, hot water with her. The woman really had him under her thumb.

"If I tell you, you can't let on you know unless *she* tells you. Then you'll know. But not before, not from me. And you can't tell any of the others. You've got to promise."

Did she have to promise? Did she owe him anything? This time yesterday, she'd have given quite a bit for him; now her emotions were barely in check. "I promise," she said with a conviction that she didn't feel—but he wouldn't know that.

"Okay," he said. "She's into...time travel."

Lenora just stood there for a few seconds just looking at him blankly and then said, "Well *woop-de-doo*. Time travel. Like we haven't already surmised we're involved in time travel up to our dog and cat asses!"

Sarcasm was seemingly lost on Frankie; he responded by merely nodding. "You must understand that intelligence has come our way that other dangerous governments in our world are interested in this kind of thing and it could change the outcome of life as we know it—and not in our favor. It goes beyond medicine now."

"That's not going to happen," replied Lenora. "I've seen the future. Trust me on this." She smirked at him and then pulled back not knowing if she was being bitchy because of his love for the Lenora of this time or because of what she really knew about the world's non-belief of any involvement with time travel. She'd seen the TV shows on the History Channel and knew all about the hubbub over the years with the interest in the paranormal. "It's a cult thing," she added. "Most people don't even care about it. Just more unproven information about a time past or a worse time future."

"Is it?" he asked. "You can say that standing here?"

"I may have been premature saying that." Lenora glanced back over her shoulder. "My dogs are dressed now," she said, not masking annoyance at the whole situation—and also not disguising the uncertainty and fear.

"Dog?" said Rex." I'll thank you to rephrase your insults in the future."

"Stop the sparring," said Divine. "This is a genuine problem on all fronts here—the future withstanding." He paused. "Remember our super-sensitive hearing?"

With that remark, suddenly Lenora, and Rex and the wolves, now in conservative college garb, found themselves standing not in front of Frankie in his office, but in an alley just outside Lenora's frame shop back in their own time. Startled and wide-eyed, they looked back and forth at each other.

"Well, we're back," said Lenora. "Anybody do something to put us through that portal again? I didn't even feel it that time."

No one answered.

Finally, Lenora spoke up. "We don't know anything more now, than we did when we were on the other side. Or in the other time zone, or time warp, or portal, or whatever the hell these things are. Were."

"And apparently," said Friar, "they—meaning the portals—can take us anytime they want if we're standing in roughly the same place of the initial occurrence."

At that, all of them took several large steps back from where they stood.

"Look on the bright side," said Rex. "At least, the clothes came along this time. That's new."

Chapter Seven

LENORA WOKE WITH A START, not knowing what brought her to such quick consciousness. Had she been dreaming? Had there been a sound in the living room, or outside her bedroom window? Was that damn Rex in cat form trying to sneak a peek at her while she slept yet again? Or more sinister, was Ned the Gorilla stalking about, looking for payback?

She couldn't put her finger on what was bothering her, but she was wide-awake and on high alert. She could see a film encasing her skin and had come to recognize this as her covering of protection. Others could not usually see it, but she could see the slight glowing form envelop her body at the oddest times. Often she would have to stop, look around, and consider exactly what the danger might be because she did not see evil behind every doorway, which was probably something she should try to do these days. It was that way this time as well. Looking around her bedroom, she could see nothing that would lead her to be concerned that an attack was imminent. Yet it was there. Something. Lingering about her in a way that she could not see or feel. Something...

Suddenly, she saw a form develop at the top corner ceiling of the room. It was gray in color and seemed to have a lightning effect running through it. What was *this* thing?

"That can't be good," she said out loud. "Okay," she said to the foggy entity—if that *was* what it was—"What can I do for you?"

It swirled slowly and moved tentatively down toward eye level and to the middle of the room in front of her bed.

She heard a strange whispering or white-noise sound as if many people were talking at once, but they was so far away or their voices so muffled that she could not make out the words. She strained her ears to hear more clearly.

Before she could blink, something crashed through the window, and a dark shape slammed into, and through, the foggy "being" before her. Lenora yelped in surprise.

The fog dissipated in seconds and the room was quiet with just her remaining wide-eyed in bed, broken glass, and a large, orange-and-white cat on its back on the floor with its legs in the air … and no swirling mass.

Rex, she thought. *You're such a pain the in the...* "What the hell, Rex! I was just about to communicate with it...I think. And what's happened to you? Why are you on your back? I thought cats always landed on their feet."

In seconds, he was a naked man in front of her. She reached to the side of the bed and grabbed her pink robe where she'd carelessly left it. Throwing it at him, she said, "God, put this on; you're just obnoxious. You need to learn to control that better. And why were you watching me? I told you to go home."

"Do you forget that I'm supposed to be guarding you?" He'd put on the robe, and was admiring himself in the mirror over her dresser. "Not my best color, pink."

She threw one of her bed pillows at him. He ducked.

"What do you think it was?" he asked. "It had lightning in it."

"Who's going to fix my window?" she demanded. "And I don't know what it was. I was about to find out. Well, I think I was anyway. There was this... this... gibberish-like sound, kinda like lots of people whispering just out of ear range."

"You know, I've seen a lot being with this family these last years—all kinds of abilities and abnormalities.... But you are something really out there." He was tying the belt of the undersized robe into a big knot.

"That's all you have to say? You turn into a cat. Your mother and brothers turn into wolves."

"Yes, yes, old history. Get a new complaint. But *you*. You're something different and special. So now you see whatever that thing was, and you hear it, too, which has to mean something." He started out of the bedroom and called over his shoulder, "Got any milk?"

"In the fridge," she called after him. "But check the date."

She closed her eyes in annoyance and yawned. When she opened them, Frankie was sitting on the bed beside her. He took her hand warmly.

His eyes were wide and he was smiling. "Hi Doll."

Though startled yet again, this time she didn't panic, but just shook her head. "Don't call me Doll." Her voice was a tired whisper and she pulled back her hand. "What do you want, Frankie? Was that you in the cloud thing? And what happened yesterday at your place? Why did we just *poof* leave? And how are you here now?"

"I don't know what happened yesterday. Or what's happened now. Things happen so quickly with this time travel mess, and I never know what's going to happen and when. I'm worried that more people will disappear if I don't do something soon. But I don't know what to do. It's got to have something to do with you and Lenora. I'm considering telling her even though she'll probably have me committed, or at the very least transferred away from her. You can see why I can't have that happen." He hung his head. "I just don't know what to do."

Lenora could see his eyes welling up, but he quickly turned his head away. Against better internal judgment, she reached out and stroked his hair. "It will work out; it will. We can figure it out."

He turned then, his brown eyes now clear, and leaned in to put his arms around her, drawing her into a bear hug. At first she was tense, but something inside her seemed to bring calmness and she relaxed into the embrace, putting her arms around his neck and nuzzling her face at his shoulder. He felt so warm and alive, so desirable. Yet she knew he wasn't actually there in any real sense. Her heart pounded as she moved her hand into his hair. Even with product in it, it felt wonderful because it was *his* hair. She kissed his neck gently, tasting the salt of a trying time he fought elsewhere. Here in her bedroom, it held the taste of passion. Her pulse quickened.

She wasn't even surprised when he pulled back and put his lips against hers. She opened her mouth slightly and allowed his tongue to search for hers. The kiss was exquisite and serene, as though this was one of many—a comfortable, perfect declaration of an ongoing love that was not touched by timelines. Sentimental sighs escaped her lips as she eagerly pushed forth for more.

"Well, now I've seen just about everything," said Rex from the doorway, glass of milk in one hand and two chocolate cookies in the other. "You are making out with air. And pretty damn impressively, I might add."

Lenora pulled back from Frankie with a start and... *poof*...Frankie was gone. Just gone. How she hated this new world of hers. She frowned hard and then spat out at Rex, "What did you do, you miserable cat?"

"What? Nothing!" he said, taking a bite of cookie and washing it down with milk. "Don't tell me. Frankie."

She threw off the covers and getting up, headed into the bathroom and slammed the door. At the mirror over the sink, she watched the tears fall down her face. This whole situation was just not fair. "I'm not going to make it through this alive," she said out loud.

"Yes, you will," said Rex from the other side of the door. "It's just a coming of age thing."

"Stop eavesdropping," she yelled. "And then get out."

She took a few minutes to put herself in order, pulling a pair of dirty jeans and a t-shirt out of the laundry basket that sat by the tub. Looking down at her shirt that said *Women Need Men Like Fish Need Bicycles,* she whispered, "Should say *Women Need Cats or Wolves Like Fish Need Bicycles.* Except my luck would be that the fish would turn into Jaws."

When she opened the door and went back into the bedroom, the lights were all out, the glass was cleaned up from the floor, and the apartment was empty. She looked out the glassless window and drew the curtains. "Looks like he followed my orders—for once."

She undressed and went back to bed. Right before she fell off to sleep, she whispered, "Frankie..." Then sleep took her.

There was a strip of light shining through the curtains when she opened her eyes the next morning. Oddly, she'd had no dreams: no images of cats turning into people, or people turning into wolves, or ghosts providing passionate kisses, or portals to times past and back. Drawing her forearm over her eyes, she thought about that and wondered if possibly the entire thing could please be a dream. There was no Charlotte the wolf bitch, no betrayal by her mother regarding crazy powers that would overtake her body just when her life was beginning to move in the right direction. Yes, a wonderful thought. It was all a dream. No will of a dead father she'd never heard about. No worries.

She snapped out of her warm calming thoughts, though, when she heard the low voices. *No, no, not again. No voices, please! They put people away for hearing voices!* She lay quietly, straining her ears to listen in the hope that it was imagination. This time, however, the voices were not whispers like the night before, just low talking, and this was more the sound of a conversation. Worse, it wasn't coming from the air around her like the night before but from her living room. Someone was in the house. And from the sound of it, there were several someones. Her body tensed and, slipping from beneath the covers and over the side of the bed, she pulled on the dirty clothes thrown on the floor the night before. Looking around for a weapon, she remembered the baseball bat that was under the bed by her night table. It was Ned's, and she'd put it there just in case he'd decided to come around again.

Now she held it in a swing mode and, barefoot, she crept toward the bedroom door, the living room directly on the other side of it. Lenora knew there was more than one individual on the other side because she could now hear them a bit better, though still not what they were saying. *I sure hope this new power to shield myself automatically goes into drive, because I don't know how to turn it on. Maybe I can suck the air out of the room like I did that one time.* Either way, nobody was going to be in her living room without her invitation.

She burst through the door screaming out a ninja yell, bat swinging.

The conversation stopped and the three men sitting around her coffee table stopped in seeming mid-sentence, eyebrows raised in sarcastic amusement.

Lenora wielded the bat. "What the hell?"

Rex was the first to speak. "Lenora, you never cease to amaze me. You play baseball, too?"

"Indoors," added Friar.

"Barefoot, and she's her own cheerleader, though the cheer needs work," said Divine.

"How did you get in my house, why are you here, and...*why* are you here?" Lenora demanded. "This is not a game. You just broke into my house!"

"Hardly," said Rex, picking up the carryout coffee he'd brought. "There's an open window in the bedroom and I just came through in my smaller version and let everyone else in through the front door." He picked up another medium-sized cup and reached up to her with it. "Here. Brought you cappuccino. All women seem to like that. It might need sugar; I only put in one."

Lenora let out a growl of sorts and grabbed the drink, taking a swig. "What the hell are you doing here? I have to go to work today. I can't be doing all this intrigue stuff all the time. I can't be going through portals and preventing... whoever...from perfecting time travel or making medical equipment. God, I hope nobody sane is listening to me."

A knock came at the door and all of them looked toward the door. No one, however, moved.

"Expecting company this early on a Monday morning?" asked Divine.

"No..." whispered Lenora. "But how bad could it be?" She paused and winced. "That was just me asking that, wasn't it?"

Nobody spoke, but Rex got up, went to the door, and looked back at all of them before opening it.

"Hey, who are you?" said Margo, looking past Rex to Lenora and the others in the room. "Party at 8am on Monday morning? Or something worse?" She walked in and turned back to Rex. "You must be Rex. Red hair was the giveaway." She held out her hand to shake.

Lenora dropped her head back against the chair in a "what next?" stance. "Hi, Margo. This is, like you said, Rex, and two of the sorta, kinda Bradley boys, Divine and Friar."

Rex added, "Not red hair, strawberry blond I believe they call it. Much more appealing. And if I have my best friend data correct, you would be the paranormal investigator—our Frankie expert."

"So you've found out for sure he's a ghost." Margo was nodding as she headed for the kitchen. "Got any milk?"

"First shelf," offered Rex. "It's good until tomorrow."

Coming back into the room with a glass of milk, she asked, "So what do these guys have to do with all that?"

"Well," said Lenora, pointing to the men, "these two are wolves, that one's a cat, and Frankie is from another time and came through a portal, or maybe he didn't, not sure about that just yet."

The men's eyes were wide and horrified.

"What?" said Lenora. "She's my best friend. I tell her most everything."

"No, that is not acceptable at all," said Divine, standing up, his muscles showing full rippling anger. "No person not of our heritage is to know about us. That's the rule."

"Oh, there are rules now? Somehow I missed that." Lenora rolled her eyes. "Another Charlotte law?"

Everyone remained quiet, but then Rex, who was back in Lenora's favorite recliner, said, "Well, it's rather an unspoken law. Safety of life kind of thing. People don't like change or those different from them. We stay quiet to stay out of the limelight."

Margo was nodding. "That's true about the safety thing. We see it all the time in the ghost world."

"See what?" asked Friar. Then he smiled. "You know, see what? Can't see a ghost and all like that?"

No one laughed.

Margo ignored Friar and continued, "Well, for what it's worth, I already know most of this, but I'm assuming from the meeting of the minds here today and the glum looks, that something else has happened that none of you can explain." Margo plopped down next to Divine on the couch. "You're cute."

"Yes, I am," he responded, as though he'd said nothing more than hello. "And how is it that you are so accepting of our truths in a world where our kind are only myth."

"Well," started Margo, "I believed werewolves were myths just like everyone else thought, but I have also found that all myths are based initially on some *real* kind of happening. Which part is real and which part exaggeration is speculative. And while yes, this is quite bizarre, it's no worse than considering the other varied violences in our world today. I have an incredibly open mind."

Divine offered her a cookie, alliance begun. Friar yawned. Rex was nodding. Lenora just sighed hard and said, "They don't like being called werewolves."

Margo nodded as she washed her cookie down with milk. "Noted. I would like to see you changed though," she added, looking at Divine.

He smiled and winked at her.

"You guys mind?" said Lenora. "The flirting can wait.

We got real troubles here." Then in a whisper, "I wish Frankie were here."

Rex rolled his eyes.

"I meant the *other* Frankie, not the one we saw earlier," she said a bit louder.

Rex turned from her, and in a dismissive tone said, "So, fellow travelers, what's the plan?"

"Fill me in first thing," said Margo. "I can't wait to hear *this*."

It wasn't long before the newly built team members were all in the same state of knowing—or *not* knowing as was the truth of things.

Margo, wiping her hands on her jeans, said, "So out of everything we do know, the only connection seems to be that Lenny is in both this world and that one. All of you are talking like the two women are the same, but it's pretty obvious to me that this is not the case. I recognize the Lenny here, but that one there doesn't sound like her *at all*. What we have here is not time travel, though—because that would mean that the same person would be in both places and have the same personality—only the time would be different. That's not the case. These women are different as night and day. So what we are probably looking at is a case of multiverse connections."

"Hmmm," said Friar. "Interesting."

Margo got up and began the pacing she always did when thinking. "Okay, let me see how I can explain this to you."

"Dearest Margo," began Divine. "You need not dumb it down for us. Friar there is in the aerospace engineering field. I'm a psychiatrist, and little Rex is a"—he began smiling and fought a smirk—"a physical education aficionado."

"Why do you always laugh at my degree? Do you know how valuable it's been in understanding the constraints of the family's changing tree?" Rex's mouth was a hard line.

"No worries, little *cuz*," said Divine. "You are always fodder for comic relief." Then to Margo, "We all have advanced degrees, so do your damnest."

Margo glanced at Lenora, who raised her eyebrows as if to say, *Wow*. The two women had degrees as well, but Margo's was a liberal arts degree and her major field of interest was theater, whereas Lenora was degreed in art history. Neither of them worked to their potential. Instead, they explored things they loved to do: Lenora painted and Margo acted in TV commercials and hunted ghosts.

Lenora spoke up before Margo could start her explanation. "I never see any of you worry about a job or work. And with those credentials, you two"—pointing to Divine and Friar—"live in a beat-up cottage in the woods."

All of them shrugged. Rex said, "We've worked, we've played, and we're wealthy enough to do it anytime and anyplace we like. No harm in that."

"Must be nice," whispered Margo.

"Anyway, Margo, please do dumb it down for me. I'm not proud," said Lenora.

Margo merely nodded. "Well. There's science behind this." She directed her comment to Friar.

He nodded.

"In a nutshell, it's like we live in one universe and there are millions of other universes that butt right up to us, and some are even on top of us. We just can't interact with them or even perceive them. But every so often they touch in just the right place, and one universe filters over onto ours. This is when you hear that people see the ghosts of dead relatives and such. It's a matter of energy placement."

Friar was wrinkling his nose. "It's not exactly like that, dear."

"In the ghost world, that's what people who think the multiverse is real believe. Well, sort of," she said, eyes wide. "I'm serious. I never really thought it held water until now."

"Need more," said Lenora. "I don't get it."

"Okay, let me say this by example. Take Gorilla Ned."

"Rather not," said Lenora, her face in a grimace.

"Ned. You know how it is here. Ned's a physically manipulative, mean drunk and all-around ass. He abuses women psychologically and physically." Margo glanced at Rex to see him nodding. "And you are you: a painter, a nice person, all-around sweetheart." She looked again to Rex, who was nodding. "Well, that's here. In this universe. But now think of another universe right next to ours that we can't see. In *that* one, Ned is a sweetheart, and you're a real wacko."

Lenora blinked, obviously not believing that such a thing could happen.

"And," said Margo, "there's yet another universe, where he is still a jackass, but you are a feeble, weak woman who doesn't have the hutzpah to throw him out like you did in this one. There are thousands of scenarios and everyone is relevant in the multiverse."

Lenora was shaking her head. "That's just awful. I mean, the possibilities are so immense I can't even get my head around it."

Friar spoke up. "I don't think that science is ready for quite so loose a translation of the multiverse theory; but I do see where you're going, and it's as good an explanation as any."

Divine added, "That's why the Lenora in that other timeline was such a bad ass, and you are so...not."

"What do you mean, not? I'm a badass. I can put a force field around me and suck the air right out of the room." Lenora's tone was snappy and a bit of resentment came through.

"That wasn't an insult...Doll," said Divine.

"Doll," whispered Lenora. Then louder, "What about Frankie? He's the same in both places."

The men all looked at each other in doubt. "Are you sure?" asked Rex. "I mean, he's clearly with her."

Lenora shifted uncomfortably in her chair and took a breath. "Well, maybe, and I suppose what I felt in my bedroom could have been...something else."

Margo was staring at her hard. "Do they know about that?" she asked.

"Spill," said Rex. "What happened in your bedroom?"

Lenora swallowed hard and looked to Margo for support. Her friend nodded that she should go on.

"In the spirit of full disclosure only. This is private stuff," she said.

Everyone sat still and allowed her the time to build the courage to say what she had to say.

"I kinda had another experience the same day I saw the scene of Frankie and that computer code guy who was with him in that room." She stopped.

"Yes?" coaxed Rex.

"I kinda had a romantic...event...and it was like in my mind, kinda, sorta." She looked at Divine. "I could have just been having a dream, or maybe I'm nuts."

Divine smiled thinly. "Then we're all nuts. And, yes, it could have been a dream, but based on everything that's happened, I'm thinking that it's your new reality. What happened?"

Lenora stalled again, taking her time and clearing her throat.

"Look, Lenny," said Rex. "We're all family here—well, except for Margo. And she's your best friend and obviously already knows. You can tell us anything now."

The other two men were nodding and no longer had the teasing looks on their faces. Things seemed more serious than she was prepared for. Especially this retelling of a most intimate experience.

Suddenly, Lenora sat up straight in her chair. "Oh!" she said. "Oh, no!"

"What, what?" said Margo.

"There was this black smoke thing in the bedroom before, floating around at ceiling level. Rex saw it, too! At first I'd thought it was Frankie."

"I did see it; it had lightning in it. I'd forgotten that fast." Rex was frowning.

"You forgot?" said Margo. "Really?"

Rex shrugged. "Lots going on, ya know?" But he squinted his eyes as though a great doubt was before him.

"What if *it* was what was...accosting me...in my...?" Lenora's voice was filled with horror. "I thought at the time it was Frankie...and then I actually saw him in that scene. I never thought about it! What if it was something else?"

Rex was contemplative. "That smoke we saw together had lightning in it and you said you heard lots of voices in a whisper."

Margo was no longer pacing, but perched on the arm of the sofa next to Divine. "What if we are talking about two different things here? Frankie in the multiverse...and something else who wants you to *think* it's Frankie."

"Why wouldn't my armor kick in and protect me from a sexual assault like that?" asked Lenora.

Divine answered, "If one of your gifts is that armor, and you use it when you're threatened, then if you feel safe or maybe find something totally ridiculous, it wouldn't manifest. Whatever came after you needed you to believe that it was something that was not a threat."

"Holy hell," said Lenora. "I'm such a putz."

"I don't think so," Margo said. "How would you know? You thought it was Frankie. You thought it was a dream. Then you thought it never happened. You were all over the place, but not once were you feeling angst that it would hurt you. Divine could be right."

"Okay, there's too many parts and pieces here. Hang on," said Lenora. She got up and went into her art studio and pulled back an easel holding a large pad of presentation paper. "Let's make a list here and see what connects."

For the next twenty minutes the group made notes on all the strange issues and anomalies. It was overwhelming in the scheme of things. There were three columns: one having changes occurring in Lenora's life, the next showed the issues in the Bradley family, and the third showed the multiverse ideas with Frankie.

lenora	Bradleys	multiverse
• Ma's death	• Thing in the attic	• Going through portal at cottage
• Finding out about my father	• lenora into the family	• Finding that Frankie and lenora from the new place in the past
• Fight with Ned	• lenora taken to Divine's cottage	• They've lost people
• Seeing Frankie all over town	• Opening of portal	• They're working on a experiment
• Ghostly things in my house		• Frankie loves that lenora but still keeps showing up here in his same persona (not a new one)
• The thing in my bedroom twice		
• Seeing the "Frankie scene"		• Coming back through portal in the alley
• Air sucking from car		
• Reading of Will		
• learning about family		
• Thing in the attic		
• Portal in woods		

Standing back to look at the chart she'd made, Lenora tilted her head in wonder. "Ya know, right now, it's all about me and the multiverse and less about any of the Bradley family. Except for the portal places that have shown up at the cottage and in the attic at the mansion—if that's what the attic thing is."

Margo nodded. "Could be they were just in the wrong place at the wrong time. Still…"

Rex, Friar, and Divine were shaking their heads no. Rex said, "If that were the case, then all of this would have happened without your getting your powers. Your powers are a big part of this, and that's because of our family heritage. Still, something big is going on with you, Lenora, and maybe this is part of what's to come of you. Maybe you're going to be some kind of portal jumper. I just can't figure out this Frankie thing."

"Multiverse traveler," suggested Divine with a smile. "I'd be drummed out of the science club for believing any of this. I'd be put into an asylum that I usually recommend people to. You," he continued, pointing at Rex, "would still be teaching college kids how to tuck and roll out of tornados. No change for you believing in something new."

Rex threw him a look of contempt. "Jealousy. It doesn't become you, cousin."

A short silence between them gave a moment for each to reflect on the new "normal." Then, very suddenly, *BANG!* came from the basement. They all jumped and stared toward the closed basement door.

"That's just my washing machine lid," said Lenora. "It's been doing that."

"That can't be good," said Divine. "I'm not up to snuff on the new washing machine technology, but I think they need human interaction to do that."

"Yeah, forgot to put that on the chart," said Lenora, now adding the strange basement to the pad on the easel. "There's something down there. It whispers and Frankie said to keep the door closed."

With the last, all three of the men got up and moved directly to the basement and opened the door.

"Yeah, I remember this from another of my visits here. I'd wager whatever's going on with her washer is part of all this," said Rex taking the lead down the stairs. "I didn't see anything when I checked down there before, though."

Lenora just sat down hard on the couch and put her head in her hands. "This is all so crazy. Just a short time ago...well, who would've thought all *this*."

Margo walked to her friend and brushed through her hair with her fingers. "Everything will be okay, my friend. Lenny...just remember that you always have me."

Lenora nodded. "I know."

They remained that way a moment, when Lenora suddenly raised her head. "I don't hear the guys downstairs."

"Me, neither," replied Margo, moving toward the basement door.

Lenora followed her, calling out, "Rex? Divine? Friar?"

No answer. Both women rushed down the stairs. No one was there. The men were gone.

Chapter Eight

"HOW DARE YOU BRING *HER* into my home!" Charlotte was furious, and she looked at Margo with contempt and revulsion. "A half-breed and a human in my only place of refuge on this horrendous planet!" Then she turned, the air swirling around her like a tornado.

Margo cowered and hung close to Lenora, intimidated and horrified.

But Lenora ignored Charlotte's transformation, finally coming into her own with her new powers and strange circumstances. This woman just did not have the clout she'd once had to intimidate her since her travel through time and space. Human to wolf was no longer a surprise. "Yes, yes," she said with a touch of impatience in her voice, "you're very intimating and all that, but with what I've seen recently, now you're just a very, very big dog with absolutely beautiful fur." Then, looking at Margo, whose eyes were still wide in fear, she added, "It's the cream rinse, I'm sure."

Margo spoke in a whisper, barely forming her words. "Yes, that's right, cream rinse. Shampoo just cleans." She reached forward with a tentative hand, as if it to touch the animal in front of her.

"I wouldn't do that if I were you," cautioned Lenora. "Big teeth and such. Remember the stories."

Margo withdrew her hand.

Lenora looked to Charlotte, noting the drool rolling from the wolf's mouth, and edged closer. "Look. I'm not here to challenge you. We women have to stick together. I know I'm supposed to need your help, but right now we all need each other's help. Three of our own are missing, and each of us here has a skill that can help get them back and figure out this whole mess. Are you with us or do Margo and I have to go for Rex, Divine, and Friar alone?"

Charlotte's three cubs, still in human form, stood by the fire, tense, but actively nodding their support for Lenora's words.

Suddenly the air around Charlotte started to spin and the wolf disappeared into it, and seconds later she was standing in front of them as a woman again. She quickly pulled her rust-colored wrap around herself and glared at Lenora.

"You're quite the whip," she began. "But I am a leader, and I do see the sense of what has to happen here." She walked to the counter that always seemed to hold some kind of liquid refreshment. Taking a glass of the purple liquid there, she said, "I don't fancy helping the D-Pack though. They are rough dogs from another line and have not been welcomed into our family for their attitudes."

"Attitudes?" asked Lenora. "Well, it's true they are quite ..." She trailed off because she couldn't really put a word to it.

One of the three cubs spoke up. "They're just young, like we used to be. Need more guidance. Like should not turn on like."

Charlotte turned on the cub. "What do you know about any of this?"

"Quite a lot, I'll wager," said Lenora. "Anyone sitting on the sidelines can see that we're going to need all the help we can get."

"Obnoxious little half-breed," snapped Charlotte as she looked back toward the two women. "I know more in my snout than you'll ever hope to know."

Lenora snapped back with an attitude of her own. "And I'll have you stop addressing me as a lesser being just because your husband slept around. That's not my fault, and I'm not here to take anything from your precious family. We've got to get it together—unless you don't care about the people...uhhhh...wolves you've lost. And cat."

Charlotte just stood for a moment and then, as if she'd not even heard Lenora's outbreak, she began to talk. "This list you've shown me is quite telling, and the bare spots are very noticeable."

Margo, a bit calmer now, asked, "How so?"

Charlotte, with difficulty, looked at the young woman and answered, "What is it again you bring to this event?"

"Oh, uh-uh-mmm," said Margo.

Lenora stepped in. "She has an understanding of the paranormal, supernatural, and the science behind it that none of us has. She instinctively knows the difference between reality and folklore, and truth and scam. She can put the pieces together. We just have to give her those pieces."

Charlotte rolled her eyes and turned her back to them. She said, "All right then. Where do we begin? I must say also at this point that I've felt things stronger from the attic. It has the whole family here on edge. Do you believe it's connected?"

Margo piped up, "Yes, it has to be. Can I take a look at the attic?"

"No!" all of them said at once.

"Well," said Lenora, "at least we agree on something. I don't think you should, Margo, because though you have the knowledge, you don't have the protection. I think there's something different here than the place at Divine's cottage. I just feel it."

"This one," said Charlotte pointing at Lenora, "and I shall go to the attic. I don't think I'll be able to go in, though."

Her hesitant manner was not lost on Lenora. Charlotte was not afraid of anything, so if anything should rattle her reserve it was the dog woman's lack of confidence in the face of the strangely compelling attic. "Okay," Lenora said, moving back toward the door. To Margo: "If we don't come back—"

Charlotte interrupted, "If we don't come back, the cubs will come for us."

Everyone nodded, understanding the timing of things.

Charlotte took the lead, walking the stairs like a queen, with her lowly servant following. Lenora's face held a grimace at her back. "Ya know, Charlotte," she said carefully, "I really am a good person, and I only have myself as far as family in the world now. I don't expect anything from you, and I really understand that the circumstances are not nice. I just would like to be casually a part of your family—not nurtured or coddled or made to feel loathsome. But to just offer me as I am to some people I've really come to like."

"You're not talking about me of course when you say 'like,'" she said without turning around. "You've taken a liking to all the outcasts. Those this family disapproves of."

"Why do you disapprove of Rex so much? He's funny and kind and tries to be likeable. He really tries."

"I don't dislike Rex. You've misinterpreted this arrangement. You are in the presence of an alpha female and I must always head the pack, lead the pack, control the pack. Rex … is difficult to control."

There was a smile in her words, though, Lenora could not see her face. She was certainly right about Rex. Lenora sighed.

They were at the top of the stairs and Charlotte turned to Lenora. "If you are to be part of this family in any way at all, you will be controlled, too."

Though Lenora didn't like it, and every nerve ending in her body wanted to scream at the woman, she only nodded. *I can deal with that*, she thought, also thinking of the ramifications of not dealing. Charlotte had already dismissed her though. She was looking toward the end of the hallway and the door that led to the small anteroom that led to the stairs going up to the attic. Both women moved forward.

Since they'd been inside the small room at the bottom of the attic stairs, they did not linger, but simply opened the door and stepped inside. Charlotte flipped the light switch bathing the room in a ghostly yellow, low-light glow. Lenora shivered and Charlotte gave her a quick frown as if to say, *Not scared already, are you?* Lenora waved her on, not reacting to the slight. Still, with the best of intentions, both women stood at the bottom of the dark staircase, and moved no farther.

Lenora could feel the hair standing up on her arms and neck, and the protective shield she'd recently acquired was already softly glowing around her body like a thick sheen. Looking at Charlotte, she could see the woman holding tight to her female human form, clenching her fists and her face taunt. They glanced at each other.

"Maybe this wasn't such a good idea," suggested Lenora in a whisper. "It feels stronger and more negative—if that's possible—than before."

"I will do what I have to do for family," said Charlotte.

"Well, so will I," Lenora snapped back. "I didn't mean—"

"Thin skin," said Charlotte.

They both fell silent and didn't move.

Lenora sighed again, drawing Charlotte's gaze. "No time like the present," she said, and started up the stairs with Charlotte on her heels.

The light in the stairway was weak and it was difficult to navigate without stumbling, but still they moved steadily forward until reaching about three-quarters of the way up.

"Wait," whispered Lenora, stopping and leaning back on the handrail. "What's that under the door—is something oozing out?" She gulped and turned big eyes back to Charlotte who was actively looking.

"The light is bad here. I'm going to turn so I can see and feel it better." She didn't wait for a response from

Lenora but disappeared into the familiar spin of air that indicated the change was coming.

Lenora just waited, no longer surprised or apprehensive of what she would see next. It was odd to say that she was now used to the process, but even so, changing into a wolf she feared would not be as horrible as what might be behind the attic door. Her heart was pounding and her skin prickling. Whatever was at the base of the door wanted to get onto her side and just needed someone to open the path for it. Would it be Charlotte and her? *Should* it be?

In the seconds it took her to think and cower from the door, Charlotte was a beautiful and ferocious cream-colored wolf. Her fur appeared so soft that Lenora (like Margo before) reached out to touch her. Charlotte growled and Lenora pulled back her hand. *No sense baiting the monkey,* she thought and then rethought, *wolf.*

Charlotte's eyes were glowing like the monsters Lenora had seen on late-night horror movies on her television set. The depth of them took her aback. It was as if there was nothing this creature could not perceive in this state of being. Lenora was thankful for that at this moment.

Charlotte started back up the stairs, a ridge of fur standing up along her spine from neck to tail in obvious readiness for a fight at first alarm. Now only two steps away, she peered at the open slit beneath the door and sniffed. Snapping her head back toward Lenora, the wolf again went into a spin. Seconds later the woman again was standing there. "There's a chemical-like substance leaking out from under the door—fog or smoke. Sulphur smell. Can you smell it, too? The devil is behind that door, child."

Both women went back down a couple steps. The devil was nothing to make light of. That thought showed clearly on both their faces. The unknown had them both cautious and the fight-or-flight response was pushing at their senses.

"I haven't had any dealings with the devil," said Lenora. "I'm not even sure I believe in the devil as a real kind of … thing …"

"Yes, this has been my thinking as well," replied Charlotte quietly.

"What made you say devil? Is that fog a sign? Is there something we can put together to have Margo research, or maybe she knows about it already. She talks about demons and Sulphur from time to time. Could there be demons in there? And what the hell would they be doing in your attic spreading all that smelly stuff around?"

"We are here now. I'm going up there and in. You wait here," instructed Charlotte.

"You think that's wise?" asked Lenora. She was squinting to see the foggy movement under the door.

"Probably not," said Charlotte, "but someone must eventually face this thing. It's in my house, so it is my responsibility."

"Okay…." But Lenora was not sure. She stood to the side as Charlotte passed by her and she lightly touched the woman's arm. "Be careful; I don't think what's in there is going to be too happy to see you. Should you go in as a wolf instead of a woman?"

Charlotte stopped. "Yes, you're right. That is my power."

She quickly swirled, and this time, Lenora was close enough to the flow of energy around the woman to feel the great power she held. It was like a whirlwind of emotion, movement, and raw aggression. There was so much stimuli coming from the change that Lenora held her breath until the wolf stood before her.

Hanging back just a bit, she watched Charlotte move up the last two steps to the attic, when suddenly the door burst open and a push of another kind of energy billowed out at them. This was sheer force—there was no particular emotion or understanding of any kind, just something that enveloped anything in its way. It was cold and hot at the same time and that was confusing. It pushed both Charlotte and Lenora back, the wind of it forcing the fur on Charlotte's body and Lenora's hair to whip back as though in a tornado wind. Lenora nearly lost her balance. She was thankful for the handrail.

Charlotte pushed forward, but then stopped short. Something else was in the terrible wind. It was small and round and had a maw that smacked open and shut. It began to suck the wolf toward the open door and Lenora could see that Charlotte was losing the battle. At the last minute Lenora grabbed onto the wolf's tail and held on with one hand as the other held to the handrail. Charlotte was howling and Lenora was screaming. They were being pulled forward with a force beyond their comprehension.

And then there were more maw creatures at the door. They seemed to balance atop each other and began to fill the entire door space, pulling the two women with the strength that neither had ever felt before. They were seconds away from being pulled in when Lenora lost the grip on Charlotte's tail. The attic creatures sucked her forward.

At that moment, from behind Lenora, three wolves and Margo flew up the stairs in an effort to rescue. But they too were being sucked forward toward the creatures. Lenora was able to grab onto Margo's sweatshirt and hold on, but the wolves—Charlotte and the three cubs—disappeared into the mix of creatures and into the attic.

The door slammed shut. Lenora and Margo stood on the stairs alone and shaking.

"Did you see 'em?" asked Margo. "Chompers. And they chomped the wolves."

"What the hell *were* those things?" demanded Lenora, pulling Margo back down the stairs. "We gotta get out of here! Those things were strong enough to take down four wolves! We were friggin lucky they didn't get us!"

Margo did not fight the race backwards. "Guess that wasn't the best rescue idea."

"No," said Lenora, "but it came in time to save you and me. So thanks. Now we have four more to save, and I haven't a clue about what to do next!"

"First thing is to get out of this house. Maybe we can go to the other wolf location in the woods that you mentioned."

"Yeah, good idea," agreed Lenora. "Though remember they wanted me to save them from their portal, too. What are all these portals about? Why do they keep taking people?" She was running down the main staircase as she turned back to Margo and called over her shoulder, "At least the other two portals we know about don't have the chompers. Where did you get that name? Is it a paranormal anomaly?"

"Haven't a clue," Margo said as they left the house. "Just felt like the old Pac-Man to me."

At the cottage in the woods, all was quiet, and aside from the hum that Lenora felt from the portal in the back room, the place was deserted. Neither felt inclined to try out the portal again and possibly end up in the middle of a strange electrical experiment, or worse, some new place that held creatures of the chomper variety. So, in poor spirits, they left the cottage and made their way back to Lenora's apartment when they could think of nothing else to do.

Once inside the apartment, however, they felt no relief. No one was there, but the remnants of prior happy times hung in the air along with a dampening of those emotions that chilled them to the bone. Something was amiss here, as it seemed to be wherever they went on this strange and dangerous day. And of course there was the basement.

"I don't like how it feels here," said Margo, her eyes sweeping the apartment for anything out of order. "It feels like it does when I'm at a heavily haunted location. Like a kind of electromagnetic energy in the air. It keeps you off kilter."

"Well, why would it seem haunted here? I mean it's not like three men disappeared from our basement or anything," said Lenora, sitting on the couch. She'd left an unfinished cup of coffee on the end table and she took a swig.

"Yuk," commented Margo. "And to answer your question, I just don't know. To be sure, though, there's been some beyond-weird stuff going on here with you since this three-month thing started and you became the unwanted pet of wolves. That in itself might cause things to feel off…or not. Not even considering the whole basement thing here."

"That's the key now, ya know. The basement is where we should be concentrating right now. We know where the other portals go," said Lenora, turning from Margo and looking toward the basement door. "We know what's in the attic at Charlotte's and what happens at the cottage. We need to know what the deal is with the basement."

"Guess that's where we're going then," answered Margo. "I have my EMF meter in the car."

"I don't think I can go down there. And no, I don't want to ghost hunt. I don't want to know. Just want to sit here and then suddenly have a real plan. Clear head or not, I still don't know what's the right thing to do." The irritation in Lenora's voice was evident, but a touch of fear slipped through as well.

"A plan for what, Doll?"

Lenora jumped. Frankie was in the room. *Thank God!* "Frankie!" she said, jumping up from the couch to greet him.

"What?" said Margo. "No fair. I still don't get to see him? After all this? Not fair."

Frankie looked at Margo with narrow eyes. "I'm right here."

"Well, not technically," said Lenora. "You were *there* in your office at the university, but *here* in this time, not so much."

"Right," said Frankie, beginning to circle the room in agitation. "I don't understand what's happening. I swear

I don't. I'm here, I'm there, there's my Lenora, there's you. And it seems we're on whole different storylines in both places. How does all this connect? Why did you and your friends disappear from my time?"

Lenora shrugged. "Don't know. And worse, they've disappeared again. And now we've also lost four more people at another portal."

Margo interjected, "Tell him about the chompers!"

Frankie looked at Lenora in question. "What's a chomper?"

"You don't want to know," she began. "But, Frankie, people are disappearing from both your time and ours. And there's some angry and hungry creatures trying to cross over from someplace to here. There's a connection, and the only common denominator is me and you."

Just then a terrible racket came from the basement. Lenora's washing machine lid was banging up and down over and over again, sending a clanging noise through the apartment.

Margo, wide-eyed, said, "And there's that."

Frankie's eyes were also wide and he moved back from the door going downstairs. "Don't go into the basement," he said in a whisper.

"That's what they all say," said Lenora.

All eyes were on the basement door.

Chapter Nine

THE COMMUNICATIONS EQUIPMENT WAS QUIET now with only Frankie sitting in front of the controls drumming his fingers on the table. He was racking his brain to figure out how all the strange anomalies were happening. Who was he in all this? Was he one person, or was he also some faction—or ghost of himself—that could be seen in another world at another time. And who was *here* when he was *there*? Who was Lenora, his love, and who was the new Lenora so like *his* version, but so different as well? Did he love them both or just one? If one, which one? They both had so many things going for them. And finally, how could he even think of that kind of thing with everything going so crazy?

The real problem was not his love but that of the disappearances of his people. Now, if his ghostly self were any indicator of still more trouble, people from the new Lenora's time were also gone. How could he handle this alone?

He shook his head and cursed to himself, though, because the person to tell would be *his* Lenora in the here and now, and he was certain that she would explode into a firestorm of blaming others for these developments. She was not like the new Lenora who strived to solve problems by facing them head on calmly (well mostly) and succinctly. How could the same two women be so different? That was easy—well, maybe not easy, but understandable in his mind in some way. These were two different women. He'd heard the new Lenora's friend, Margo, talk of the multiverse with all kinds of timelines happening at the same time, and that was the story that made the most sense. Still, how did that connect to him and the experiment he was working on? That was about capturing and changing particles so that quantumly they could be manipulated into medically improving a person's physiology. The other Lenora had said that he and she were the keys because there were two of her and he was only one person in two places—if one counted his ghost as part of him and not an independent being.

So were they changed as quantum physics might suggest? Was this like Schrodinger's cat, where when unobserved the cat was both alive and dead? Was he both because of the experiments? And what of Lenora, supposedly changing in three months? What was that all about? What was she changing into? Did that have to do with what he was doing here? He only worked with test tubes and particle separators. Had he set off a chain reaction of some kind?

And now...chompers. What on God's green Earth were they? Had he further created a monster with this line of research? Or somehow opened yet another multiverse portal to a world of violent, killing monsters? This had been the first time he'd heard of them. Why would he not have even suspected this kind of negative outcome when trying to create a new principle? The chompers put a different, more deadly kink in the whole strange story, though: time manipulation, other universes and portals, two Lenoras, humans who turned into wolves, powers for the new Lenora beyond what he could imagine, himself a ghost and a person at the same time, and now killing things called chompers. (And aside, wasn't it interesting that he had the full memory capacity of his ghost self, even though he didn't remember actually interacting at the time he was there on the other timeline?) He wrung his hands knowing that he was close to lunacy. Even if he *did* tell his Lenora, she wouldn't believe him.

As if on cue, his Lenora threw open the door to the office. "Where have you been?" she asked with a worried tone in her voice. "I've been looking everywhere for you! Two more people have gone missing—this time from, of all places, the cafeteria!"

"Sit down," he said, patting a chair near him. "I have something to tell you, and I just ask that you suspend your beliefs for a moment and truly listen."

"Sounds serious," she said. "Does it have to do with the missing persons and our research?"

"I think so," he said. Then he told her the tale—leaving out, of course, his mixed emotions for the new Lenora. That would have no relevance, at least that's what he knew he must tell himself.

When he'd finished talking and answering any question he could, Frankie sat with his head resting on his arms, tired and frustrated, trying to think of the next steps.

His Lenora was, however, not in the same state of mind. "You can't possibly believe that this other woman who looks like me is able to willy-nilly cross time barriers, and that she has a protective coating. And wolves? This is psychosis, Franklin. Further, none of this has anything to do with our experiment or the disappearance of our technicians. It sounds like fantasy, a fabricated emotional response to pressures you are unable to face. I'll spend no more resources traipsing about to investigate your strange… experiences. You should check yourself in with that new psych doc. I've heard good things about him, and you need to be on task and not breaking down like this." Then she stood and walked out.

So, Frankie thought once she was gone, *I am on my own*. He'd expected her to be suspicious of all the varied components of the story, but he'd not expected to be totally dismissed. Fantasy? Fabricated emotional responses? Well, to be honest, there *was* more than one stumbling block to the whole mess that might be construed as psychologically unnerving. But this was not a fantasy anyone in their right mind would dream up. A bit of anger tipped his conscience at her lack of trust and respect for him. Still, he understood the pressure she was under—and of his own—and no relationship worked one hundred percent of the time.

Just then a knock sounded at the door, which then slowly cracked opened. Rex peeked into the room around the side of the door. "Anybody home?"

Frankie was on his feet in a second and pulled open the door. "You're back!" Then he noted their attire: Rex in knicker-type pants that were way too tight, and Friar and Divine in khakis and starched shirts that were way too big. Frankie frowned. "I see that whole naked-when-traveling thing is still happening."

Rex spoke up first. "This time I lost mine, too. It was like something pulled them off me. Very…uncomfortable." Looking around, he continued, "Nice digs here, professor."

Frankie barely heard him. "Where's Lenora and Margo? We were about to go in the basement the last time I saw them—you three had disappeared. And they'd found out about chompers. And then the next thing I knew, here I was again in my time."

The other three just looked at each other. "Chompers. Can't be good," whispered Divine.

Rex said, "Lenora and Margo didn't follow us to the basement, so they're still in the apartment as far as I know. But if I know anything at all about Lenora, that won't be for long. She's sure to jump head on into trouble. Chompers. Oh, yes, that sounds like something she would involve herself with."

"Regardless," said Divine, "we need to get back somehow—there's too much going on at home to be stuck here."

Friar perked up. "Maybe we could go back to the office where we were during the first time we came here. Something whipped us back to our time from there. Maybe it will do it again."

"Or," suggested Rex, "it could send us someplace else…some chomper place…or worse."

"This is true," said Frankie. "There has to be a portal to Charlotte's attic—a bad one—another one to Divine's place, the roadway at Lenora's frame shop where you ended up last time, and now one in her basement that is not on either plane. Who knows where or when one will pop up next?"

"That's what we need to deal with," said Divine. "We need to know why these portals are popping up. It does seem to be like Friar mentioned: All portals seemingly begin at Frankie's small office space. If, that is, we don't look too closely at the attic or the basement—that throws a wrench into any real theory."

"So what exactly are you and your femme fatale doing there in your office?" asked Rex.

"As I said before, we're working on a medical application using electromagnetics. This is a research university. What we do shouldn't cause any of this," said Frankie.

"Maybe our Lenora's change has something to do with it after all," offered Rex. "She might be using some kind of magnetic energy that can allow her to manipulate time. And she somehow tapped into the amount of energy you were using in your timeline. She just doesn't know what her power is or how to control any of it. I mean I was in a car when she sucked all the air out of the interior. She's clueless to it all, and I doubt she'll be any help in figuring it all out."

"You know," said Friar, "as crazy as that sounds, that does seem to make sense. She's attracted to magnetic fields and they to her. The armor around her is a force field—I bet it's got magnetic properties. And Margo measures those fields, remember, so we have her on our team. So wherever an electromagnetic field shows up, that might be where Lenora builds a portal—with her powers. Without knowing it."

"Powers," began Frankie. "Just what kind of power would that be and how would it have any value?"

The other three men shrugged.

Just then the door opened and the Lenora from this past time walked in. "Franklin," she began, "I'm sorry I was so hard on you. This has been difficult for all of us, and we need to get to the bottom of it. I just don't see—"

She stopped short staring at the four men looking back at her. Their eyes were wide.

"Wow," whispered Divine. "Different, but the same."

Rex and Friar were nodding. Except for the heavily applied red lipstick and severely pulled-back hair, they were looking into the face of their casual artist Lenora from the future.

"Surreal," said Rex.

Lenora tilted her head in question, glancing at the new men and then back to Frankie. "Your friends are ..."

Frankie looked startled, "Oh, yes...these are my friends I was telling you about."

Lenora frowned and squinted her eyes in suspicion as she looked at the three men.

Frankie nodded to each man. "Rex, Divine, and Friar." He paused. "From the future." He paused again. "And they're wolves."

Rex cleared his throat and gave Frankie a glare.

"Oh," said Frankie, "except him. Rex is a cat. A really big one. Annoying."

Rex stepped forward. "Not all that annoying." He offered his hand to Lenora. "Charmed."

Reluctantly, she raised her hand, but then pulled it back. "No. You cannot think for a moment that I would believe any of this."

Frankie shrugged in an I-told-you-so motion. The three men just looked at each other in question.

Friar whispered to Divine, but it was loud enough for all to hear. "How many people are we going to tell about us—it's against the rules you know."

Frankie shot back, "It's not like she's somebody new—not really. She's the same Lenora, you know."

"Okay, okay," said Lenora, "enough is enough. We've got real problems here and you fellows are playing fantasy. I'm at a loss to understand why, but it is definitely not proper etiquette in situations of peril."

"Maybe you should change," offered Frankie to the men. "That would be irrefutable evidence she couldn't argue with."

Divine and Friar were shaking their heads. "No way," said Divine. "Charlotte is already fierce about this, and us springing our secrets on innocents will infuriate her more. We do not need that kind of grief."

"You do it, Rex," said Friar. "Nobody cares what happens to you."

"Well, thanks a lot," replied Rex, "but as it happens I *do* believe I'm the best candidate, especially since the two of you will come out of the whole thing naked. No one should be subjected to that."

"I think it's time all of you left the campus." Lenora was dismissive now and walked to a desk in the corner of the room. "I've got work to do, and so does Franklin. Have your fantasies during your own time and away from good working people." She looked back at the four men, who were standing in a line looking back at her.

Suddenly, Rex threw the area near him into the swirling air that the Lenora of the future found so uncomfortable. Seconds later, he was standing in a pile of his clothes looking like the orange-and-white striped and horribly huge cat.

Lenora fainted, dropping to the floor as though in slow motion.

"Yep," said Divine. "She's exactly like our Lenora in some ways."

"She even faints with style," added Rex.

Charlotte's attention, usually alert in any state, felt lethargic and unfocused. Her memory was fuzzy and she couldn't remember where she was or why she was. Looking down at her naked body, she wondered where her clothes were— she always knew where her clothes were when she changed back to human. Never did she have to consider her whereabouts or her physical demeanor, but things were different here. Her skin looked pallid instead of fresh and vibrant. Her brain was buzzing, and her eyes were unaccustomed to the smoke-filled room. But no, it wasn't smoke—not exactly—but some kind of unclean air that had the taste of an electrical charge. She saw bits of lightning and fizzes of charge around her. Then she remembered the attic and tried to sit up straight ignoring the buzzing in her brain and the ache in her head. Weakness was not something she'd felt for hundreds of years and it was debilitating. Still, she pulled herself up to survey the situation.

There above her was a darker cloud within the already gray air, with even more charge to it, and it was over top one of the cubs, a piece of it swirling down and covering his head. It was a mass with suctions and it appeared to be taking his life force from him. Charlotte didn't know how she knew this, but she could feel his energy slipping away, and when he died, she could feel his pain die along with him. There were no injuries to his body, no blunt force or trauma to his being. He just had no more essence. Loss of all energy. All life force. He was free, but he was also gone forever. The cloud swirled quickly, as though in triumph, and moved to the next cub still lying quietly as though sleeping. *What is it?* she screamed in her mind as she again fell back into a deep sleep.

"You can't shut me out," Margo said. "I need to be a part of whatever plan we come up with because, well, I just do. You can't do this alone."

"But you don't have any power to protect yourself. I have this shield thing. Nothing can get at me when it's up." Lenora was standing over Margo in the kitchen trying to bully her into listening to reason.

"Just stop trying to convince an inconvincible person, and come up with some way that I *do* have the same protection," said Margo, without hesitation. "There's got to be a way to extend your shield. I mean, that's the way superheroes work."

"Superheroes? You're kidding, right? That's true fantasy, and this is not that. Oh, way beyond not that. Earth to Margo!" Lenora threw up her hands. "I don't have a clue how it works for me, let alone extend it to you."

"Well, we're sure running out of time, so stop whining and start thinking of a way to test it," replied Margo.

"How? It only comes when there's danger. And when there's danger…that's just not the best time to do a trial run, ya know?"

"True," relented Margo. "Maybe a moderate trouble?"

"I don't think that will work either because I'll know that it's not a real trouble and then the power skin won't work."

Both women just stared at each other, both thinking hard to find ideas that might prove useful for a test. Disgusted, Margo got up and went to the window pulling the curtain aside to look out absently to the back alley behind the house as she thought.

She coughed. "Uhmmmm."

"What?" asked Lenora, now sitting with her head in her hands at the table.

"What about Gorilla Ned?"

Lenora glanced up. "What about him?"

"Well," began Margo, "suppose we use him as a test. When he starts his stuff, I could hold on to you and see if I'm protected."

"You're kidding, right? I'm not going hunting for the gorilla. That makes no sense. And it would cause more problems than solving issues."

Just then a pounding came at the back door—a loud, angry pounding.

Lenora jumped and then looked at Margo. "No. That's *not* him. Are you psychic now?"

"Not exactly. I saw him sneaking around the side of the house. Why waste an opportunity, Lenny. Let's try it on him. What harm can it do?" Margo's eyes were wide with invitation.

The banging came again. "I know you're in there, Lenora," yelled Ned. "And that bitch friend of yours, too. Open the door or I'll break it in this time."

Lenora dropped her head with a loud sigh. "Oh, okay, Margo. But stay slightly back in case it doesn't work. I don't want you getting hurt."

Both women were looking down to see the sheen of power encircling Lenora's body and they smiled. Margo said, "That is so friggin' cool." She grabbed Lenora's hand and then both their smiles got bigger as they watched the sheen wash over to Margo's hand, up her arm and then over her body.

More banging at the door.

"Shall we answer?" said Lenora sweetly to Margo. "Our favorite gorilla seems to want to see us."

"By all means." Margo pulled open the door with her right hand as she held tight to Lenora with her left. There in the doorway stood the gorilla of a man: Ned. He had a snarl on his face and he smelled of alcohol.

"I do believe that you are breaking the orders the court gave you to stay away from this property and me," said Lenora, her voice even and cool.

"Yeah, Gorilla," added Margo. Her much louder voice, however, had a snarky I-dare-you quality to it.

"You bitch," barked Ned, as he swung at Margo.

Lenora pulled Margo back a step, just as Margo raised her own fist to slam back at the one coming at her. Margo's fist did not touch Ned, yet he fell backward with great force, falling off the back porch and landing on the cement beyond. He moaned and then pulled himself up, narrowed his eyes at the women, and then limped away out into the alley.

Lenora pushed the door closed.

Margo was dancing around and laughing. "PK, PK, PK!" she was singing. Then she started to do a suggestive jive with her hips. "We got PK, oh, we got PK..."

Lenora was still and silent. It was not beyond her that something important had just happened. Not only could she extend her shield when the need arose, but also she was capable—as was anyone touching her—of psychokinesis. This was the ability to move objects by mental ability alone—PK for short in Margo's world. If she had known that when the chompers had taken Charlotte and the cubs, she might have been able to close that door before they'd been sucked through it. The powers she was developing were problematic in so many ways she could hardly breathe. And this one was just another to keep track of. *Frankie, where are you?* He would know what to do. But who was she kidding? He had troubles of his own with his people missing and *his* Lenora.

"Hey," interrupted Margo, "wake up there. Don't you see what this means? I can fight right alongside of you as long as I'm touching you. We can make a plan. We can go down in the basement and find the guys and then go back and kick some chomper ass."

Lenora was shaking her head. "You don't understand, Margo. Yes, this is a good thing we've found out. But there's more to it. First, we don't know what's downstairs and where that portal leads. Second, I felt the energy around the chompers, and I felt the energy that Charlotte had. Charlotte is one powerful creature. Much more so than I could ever have imagined. Much more so than me, even with these powers. But the chompers had more power. And if they get *her* power…our plan has to be really good and really well thought out, Margo. Or we all die. And not just us. I'm thinking all mankind. On this planet, in this time anyway. I don't know what it has to do with Frankie and what he's doing in the past; I know it's connected, but I don't know why or how. I just know we have to get to all of them before these chompers get to any more of us."

Margo was listening intently now. "Yes, so that means we need to find out how to find the guys without accidentally finding the chompers. Yet if we don't go for the chompers, we don't save Charlotte and the cubs."

Both women sighed. Margo said, "We need a plan."

"Okay," offered Lenora. "How about this? You saw the first *Poltergeist* movie?"

Margo was nodding, "Of course …"

"We can tie a rope around me with the other end tied off up here with you. I go downstairs and check things out. If something goes wrong, and the rope goes taut for too long, you drag me back. You're strong and could do it."

"We're kinda back in the superhero talk," said Margo. "That was a good movie and all, but …"

"I know. It was a movie. Still...do you think it might work? Could be a good test," said Lenora.

"Yeah...but what if you disappear and I can't pull you back and then I'm stuck here not having any powers for anything and *all* of you are gone?" asked Margo.

"Well," answered Lenora. "There is that."

Chapter Ten

THE ROPE TIED AROUND LENORA'S WAIST was nice and snug. Margo never ceased to amaze her with her wide variety of odd skills—the knot-tying one apparently from her sailing lessons on the lake. It was not coming loose anytime soon. Taking down the rope swing in the back yard hadn't been easy, especially with the rickety ladder from the shed. Still, they'd managed, even though both felt the time slip away with all the small interruptions. *Poltergeist* movie or not, no one on that set had asked where the rope came from or how it was tied, or how long it had to be. Well, the questions were endless in that way. But here they were: standing at the basement door, one end tied to the front doorknob—the whole door and frame would be pulled from the wall before the rope gave way—and Lenora about to open the door to whatever lived and breathed in the basement.

Her tools, as far as she knew, were her outer protective skin, PK, the ability to suck the air out of the room—which she didn't know how to use—and who knew what else? In reality, that wasn't much in the face of things. But it was all they had. So. *Now or never*, as the saying went. The women hugged.

Margo held tight to her hands. "Now remember. Keep slack in the rope. If it goes taut and stays that way for over one minute, I'm pulling you back, unless I can hear you over the walkie-talkie." She clipped the communicator to the waistband of Lenora's jeans. "Don't drop the talkie."

Lenora nodded.

"Keep the voice button activated so I can hear everything that goes on. If I need to talk to you, I'll key the unit and you'll hear the crackle. Then you can switch it. You know how it goes."

Lenora nodded. "I'm ready. I'm psyched." But she wasn't. She was thinking about everything that could go wrong, because she couldn't really think of anything that could go right.

Margo was patting her arm now. "Everything's going to go fine."

Lenora still nodded and opened the basement door. The light switch was already set to on. She stepped down into the gloom.

It was strange, but as she went down the stairs, she didn't feel any particular notion of doom or prickling of the hair at her neck. The armor was working and she could see the slight sheen of it in the dim light; but other than that, it was nothing more than her going down to do her laundry. She remembered briefly that she'd not done her laundry for quite some time and pretty soon, she'd either have to do it or buy more underwear. Such was the case when you were afraid of ghosts in the basement—if you were indeed afraid. It could be that she just hated doing laundry. Yes. That sounded right. She dismissed the thought.

At the bottom of the stairs, she stopped and looked around. At first she saw nothing. But at the very back of her brain, she thought she could hear voices coming from the far corner of the room. They sounded insistent and worried, yet they were merely whispers. Lenora took in a breath and closed her eyes. Very quietly she began to meditate, taking her mind down to a field of flowers and reaching out to a group of people who were all wearing lab coats. They were waving her over. Their eyes held fear. She didn't move right away, but instead, pulled their images closer in her mind and singled out one woman. She pulled that likeness of the woman closer, keeping the flowers around her. Little by little the woman came closer, and as she did, the fear on her face lessened, replaced by a quizzical look of wonder.

"Hello," Lenora whispered. "Who are you?" She was careful not to move or speak loudly. She didn't want to frighten the woman.

The woman, slight in form, tilted her head and looked around. "This is much nicer," she said. "How am I here and there and nowhere all at once?"

"I don't know," said Lenora. "But let's try to figure that out. Right now, you are in my meditation. This is my field of flowers. I come here to relax my mind. In reality you are a form in a crowd of forms in my basement—kind of ghostly."

"Yes, we were whisked away from the university when we turned on the machine…and then we were brought here. Where are we?" Fear was beginning to return to the woman's eyes.

"No, no, don't look around, just see the flowers right here," instructed Lenora. "Be here in the field with me." The woman calmed again.

"You are safe in the field and also in my home in my basement. I'm trying to figure out how to get you back to your home now. You just need to stay calm and keep the others calm too. How many of you are there?" asked Lenora, now handing the woman a small bouquet of flowers for her to focus on.

"We're about fourteen now," said the woman, gazing at the flowers in her hands. "We were ten; then more came. Everyone is terrified."

"I understand that. I would be too. Have them meditate if they can. Bring them here to the field. And know that there are those of us trying to get you back, and we won't give up. I promise." Lenora was looking at the woman, but something drew her attention to the peripheral space around her. A door in the back of the basement that had not been there before was now there. She squinted at it.

The woman, seeing Lenora look behind her, took in her breath sharply and dropped the flowers. "No, don't look there. Don't go there! There's danger there! We stay as far away from there as we can. We don't want it to know we're in here!"

Lenora could feel her body shield strengthen, its form thickening and spreading over her body. She touched the woman and slowly raised her hand sending her back to the others in the field and then let herself come up from the meditative state. Back to the present, she noticed the agitated group at the corner was softly moving now, and Lenora hoped that indicated a calmer state for the group of missing people. She hoped she could save them like she'd promised.

The new door was still there—it had come along from the meditation and it was bulging outward. Lenora started when she heard the walkie-talkie crackle and immediately reached down to switch it to receive.

"Lenny, you there? What's happening?" Margo's voice was scratchy.

"Yes, I just meditated into the murkiness we saw down here and it's the people from the university back in Frankie's time. They are scared to death, and I told them we'd save them." She paused and whispered to herself, "Hope we can do that...." Then back to Margo, "But that's not the bad part. There's another door down here, that's not *really* a door, that's in my *real* basement. And it's got some of those chomper things behind it—I'd bet any amount of money. It's bulging. The question is whether this is a new chomper place or the same one from Charlotte's." She switched the walkie-talkie back for Margo to talk.

Margo said, "Okay, so come back up and we can regroup. Switching over."

"That's silly. There's nothing to regroup. We go ahead with the plan. That's what the rope is for. I go in the door. I see what's there. You pull me back. Over."

"I don't like it," said Margo. "I'm not getting a good vibe. We coulda been wrong. I mean, I know we were wrong. The rope thing won't work. Over."

"Yes, it's gonna work. I'm going in. Here I go. I'm leaving the talkie on so you can hear me." With that, Lenora moved slowly to the pulsing and bulging door. Its movement seemed to have a heartbeat. "Frankie?" she whispered out loud. "I hope you're around, cuz I need your support now."

Rex, human again, stared down into Lenora's face as he softly slapped her cheeks. "Wake up, dear one. Time to face your nightmares."

Frankie pushed him away. "Don't let her wake up to you. She'll faint again." Then he said to Lenora as he saw her stir, "Doll, come on, now. Come to. We've much to do before it gets to be too late."

Lenora opened her eyes. "Where am I?"

"Original opening," whispered Friar, and the others glared at him. He raised his eyebrows and shrugged. "Whatever."

Lenora suddenly sat up straight and pushed Frankie away. "I saw—I saw...no, no, couldn't have been." She looked at Rex. "You. You were a...no, I must have been dreaming...or...delusional."

Rex slowly shook his head. "No, nothing so simple, I'm afraid, Ms.—Doll. I indeed am the great Rex cat."

Divine snickered, and Rex gave him a dirty look.

"Don't for one moment think that I don't know what's going on here," snapped Lenora.

Divine and Rex hung their heads in disbelief, and Frankie slapped his forehead. "She actually sees the change and refuses to believe it. She is not like our Lenora; this is a surety," said Rex.

Lenora, uncertain, but still firm, said, "You've drugged me. What I saw is not possible."

Frankie interrupted, gently taking her hand, "Now, Doll ..."

Lenora seethed and said through her teeth, "Don't. Call—" She pulled back her hand and scuttled back from him on the floor.

"Yes, yes, dear—don't call you Doll. I won't. What I need to tell you, though, is that what you saw is true. No one drugged you. Think back. When would something like that have happened? My story to you is true. These men are from the future and they are also shapeshifting beings." Frankie reached forward again. "We have a problem here, and it has to do with our machine. These people are involved because of it, and our people have disappeared too. You need to settle in your mind that this is real so we can figure it all out. Many lives depend upon it."

Lenora didn't pull her hand away this time, and instead used the connection to help pull herself up. She looked suspiciously at Rex. "Do it again," she ordered.

Rex raised his eyebrows. "Would you like fries with that?" he asked.

Frankie and Lenora frowned. "What?" Frankie asked.

"Oh, never mind," said Rex, barely above a whisper as he disappeared into his foggy change mode. Seconds later a cat stood before the group.

"That's a big cat," said Lenora, but she was tottering on her feet. Frankie grabbed her. "I'm okay," she said. "I'm not going to faint this time. This is no different than... than...a discovery of some kind."

Friar and Divine rolled their eyes. Divine said, "Rex, a discovery.... I'd not have thought to put it that way."

"Okay," said Lenora. "Come back now, cat."

Rex spun, and in moments, he was a person again.

Then Lenora spun toward Divine and Friar. "Now you do it."

"Has spunk," said Friar to Divine.

"Spunk? No. She's rude. No Doll. We're not turning

for you. We're not here for your whims. We're here to solve a problem," said Divine. It didn't take a genius to tell that both Friar and Divine were losing patience with the Lenora of this time.

"Stay calm," suggested Frankie. "We do indeed have a problem, and there's no time for the formalities." He pulled Lenora around to look her squarely in the eye. "You just have to believe the rest by trusting me. The Lenora from their time is in trouble back there, we are sure, and it all relates to this time. And our people are in her basement."

Everyone was nodding at Lenora.

Rex spoke up. "I don't know about everyone else, but having two Lenoras is confusing in conversation. Let's call this one Lenora and our girl Lenny—since that's what Margo calls her as her best friend. It will make things easier. And to everyone here, let's remember that neither of them likes to be called Doll." The men laughed, lightening the mood. Except for Lenora. They were surprised to hear that she could growl.

"All right, let's get to the machine and check the data yet one more time, and I will bring Lenora up to speed." Frankie led them out of the office with Lenora looking back at the men following as though they would pounce on her at any moment.

Lenora was standing in front of the pulsing door and she could feel her own energy skin pulsing right along with the door. It caused her brain to pulse as well, and it was so loud she thought she'd run screaming any moment. But at that last second she felt Frankie at her elbow and she glanced over at him.

"I'm here," he whispered.

Oddly, she could hear him perfectly well over the pulsating whooshing inside her head. She took a deep breath. He was filmy and see-through and not like he'd been at her apartment earlier. But he was here with her and that was all that mattered. She remembered that this was how it had begun with him being ghostly there and not there. *Wait. No, that's not how it was. He was always right there. Maybe a little ghostly from time to time but never this…transparent. This is different.*

"I'm here," he said again, more insistent this time. "We'll do this together."

"Do what?" she returned, now feeling confused in her mind and looking between him and the strange breathing door before her. "Oh…the door. What's behind it, Frankie?"

"I think it's just energy, and you've got that covered. You do. You are protected by your energetic coating on your body, and you have, of course, me…."

She turned to him again, feeling a strange desire rise up in her chest, one so warm and seductive that she wanted to swoon, to fall to the ground pulling him on top of her, stripping herself of the energy field and all her clothing, opening herself to him permanently and forever. She started to sink to the ground and Frankie came along with her. She allowed his hands to explore her, to slip through her armor and beneath her clothing. It felt so enchanting.

He teased her, moving from spot to sensitive spot as she now lay on the floor. He was becoming more solid now, and his touch was more insistent and probing—inside her, right through her jeans, it seemed, his tongue right beneath her shirt. His mouth was covering hers, and her pleasure escalated.

She moaned ever so softly. Then suddenly she heard the radio crackle, over and over like someone was keying the mike with frenzy, and this was pushing at the edges of her mind.

"Ignore Margo," Frankie whispered in her ear and then took over her mouth again and resumed a pulling on that place between her legs as well. He would manipulate and raise her almost to eruption and then let her sink slowly down again so that her breath would come faster and faster and then slowly rebuild when he pulled away; then he would start over again. It was the most heavenly, delicious emotion that had ever touched her. Her energy field around her was all but gone now. She spread her legs more widely to give him easier access. He complied hungrily.

But the infernal radio's clicking kept pushing at her mind. She could hear it interfering: *click click click click.* What was Margo thinking? *Oh, just let me answer her so I can get back to it, to us,* she thought to Frankie, and she pulled back from him, even as he struggled to keep that from happening. In seconds her force field bounced back into place, thicker and stronger than she'd ever felt, and the Frankie before her burst into a black cloudy mass and dissipated. The door—and her brain—stopped pulsing.

Sitting there on the floor now, shame rising red on her face for no one to see, but for her to feel, brought tears to her eyes. She switched the radio to speak. "Margo, I'm all right. You saved me. The foggy thing tried to trick me into thinking it was Frankie. I was almost a goner. Clicking over to you."

"I knew I should have come along," spewed Margo into the radio. "Did you open the door? Did you see it? Over."

Lenora keyed the radio. "No, it came outside the door and tried to get me on this side. I can also see the people—the good people—swirling around agitated at the other end of the basement. They must have seen what was happening as well. That was too close, Margo. I'm going to have to be more careful. That thing is smart. I gotta go through that door though. And I'm going right now. Get ready to pull me back."

The door was before her, silent as a stone—the way doors should be. But there was still something fuzzy about her senses that told her something behind it was much worse than anything she might think. It was worse than Gorilla Ned for sure. She remembered clearly the horrific creatures that had turned into one maw and sucked Charlotte and the cubs into its vast wilderness—or whatever landscape was beyond. It was a safe bet that this was the same thing. The other portals, though frightening in their swirling masses, were just that: swirling masses of energy. She'd been scared, yes. But only of the unknown, the fear of what was inside the turbulent winds of space. This was different. This was very much like watching television and yelling at the actress not to open the door—or to go into the basement with a rope tied around her waist that would never work, so she'd better have a backup plan that the audience wouldn't see coming. Gee. What the hell would that be?

"Well," she said out loud so Margo could hear her, "no time like the present." She reached forward and grabbed the handle to pull open the door and expose the creatures she hoped were not behind. But nothing happened. Lenora struggled with the door, jiggling the handle and pulling with all her might. It didn't budge.

She could hear the clicking of the radio, so she said, "No go, Margo. It won't open. Ideas?" Then she clicked the radio over.

"Well, this is anticlimactic, isn't it? How do we get it open?" Lenora could hear the tapping of Margo's pen on the table where she was obviously sitting to monitor her. She did that when she was nervous or stumped. *Annoying character trait, but we all have them,* she thought, considering her own habit of pacing to think, one she shared with her friend after all these years together.

"There doesn't seem to be a lock or anything like that," Lenora noted, scouring the knob. "And I don't see anything that would be a secret lever."

Just then she glanced behind her at the white cloudy fog that held the fourteen people from the past. It was swirling and moving forward inch by inch to her. As it moved, tendrils from the cloud reached out in her direction, swirling, so that all she needed to do was to reach out with her fingertips to receive the cloud. Her protective covering wavered and some of it was drawn from other parts of her body to her hand, to the fingers, and it was reaching out to the moving cloud. It looked like taffy stretching out into the air. She reached forward and the two forces met, sending a blast of energy into her and thrust her back against the door, its knob now pushing into her back.

The knob was hot and pulsing again, seeming to respond to this new energy source that was coupling with her own. She could feel the personalities and the energies of those she'd met earlier in the basement and knew they were risking a lot to help her. They were afraid. Still, they forged forward to help her do what she knew she must do.

Lenora called out to Margo to update her and prepare her to pull her free if needed. She grabbed the doorknob and pulled. This time it opened easily; in fact, it flew open and a torrent of hot, tornado-like air blew out, knocking Lenora nearly off her feet. The wind was fierce and she struggled to see what was behind the entranceway.

"I've got to go inside," she yelled out. "I can't see from here! There's too much swirling portal activity. If it's a portal I won't go in it! I'll stay at the edge!"

Edging to the door, she grabbed the frame and peered inside. There was a lump on the floor not three feet away from her but she couldn't see what it was. But suddenly it moved and Lenora recognized the form of a person. The person reached up, stretching a withering arm toward her. Then she saw who it was: Charlotte!

Lenora was only a step away from her, but it felt as though she were pushing back a freight train to move even an inch forward. Still, she pushed on. She could hear Charlotte moaning and crying now, and the form was wavering as a chomper slid down from the ceiling and attached itself to the woman's head. Charlotte wailed, the sound being part human and part wolf bellowing out a last howl.

"Not today," whispered Lenora as she threw her hand out in front of her and up at the chomper. With her mind she pushed out and then pulled in her own breath. The air began to cool and then to leave the room, a whooshing sound whining through the air. Lenora reached out, grabbed Charlotte's arm and pulled her to her. "The others," she called out over the rushing air. "Where are the others?"

"Dead," replied Charlotte, sinking into Lenora's arms.

The white cloud behind her began to pull her back and the rope at her waist, now taut, was also jerking her backward. Lenora was tiring, but she had to hold on to the air of the room, but still leave herself and Charlotte enough to get out. When it seemed that not another breath could be had, there was a loud popping sound. The two women fell to the basement floor, the door slammed and disappeared, and fourteen people seemed to fall from the ceiling to the floor of her basement.

Silence.

Chapter Eleven

FRANKIE LOOKED DOWN AT HIS SHOES, trying not to anger his colleague yet again. She was always angry these days.

"This is just not possible," Lenora was saying to the men. "There is no precedence for DNA to be within the electromagnetic containment field. None. That's like mixing apples and oranges—or mating a dog with the grass it pees on. Can't happen. At least it shouldn't happen." She was peering into a microscope and comparing it to readings on a small machine next to her.

"And yet," replied Frankie, "there it is. Think for a second. It's not that far out of the realm of possibility. Our research has shown before that electromagnetism can adversely affect the brain—especially in women. It can make some suicidal."

Lenora turned to him with a frown. "So you're pulling women out, saying they become suicidal when faced with too much electromagnetism? I believe the research indicates anyone—not just females—can have that happen." She began to pace, and Rex, Friar, and Divine smiled as they noted the similar behavior from their Lenny when she was formulating a theory or plan or appropriate dinner locations.

"Franklin," Lenora began. "This is not just a formulation that adversely affects a person's brain. This is an actual DNA strand inside the magnet. How do you explain how it got there? And what are the ramifications of something so bizarre? Why are we even able to see it?"

All the men said at once, "Portals."

Lenora just shook her head. "And how did the DNA get there, and why does it cause portals?"

Divine stepped forward to look at the data. "You can be sure that Lenny is involved—and her change. Otherwise, none of this would be happening."

"About that," said Lenora. "I don't understand why she even exists. She is me. But yet she is not me. Franklin has been babbling about the multiverse, and I'm not entirely dismissing it, but you can clearly see that it's not a sustainable theory, can't you? None of this is plausible." She was looking directly at Frankie as if the other three men were not there.

"Well," interrupted Rex, not paying attention to her frown, "that's really neither here nor there. The fact is we now have portals and two of you. Remember the saying: When all probable issues are taken away, the one that remains holds the answer—or something like that."

"And we also have chompers—how does your quotation apply to that?" asked Divine.

"So the question is not whether the portals exist or how they got here, but how do we control them?" posed Frankie. "I think we need Lenny."

"No," said Lenora, "we do not need her. You have me. I'm the one with the scientist's mind. I'm the one working on the theories to improve mankind."

Frankie took her hand and pulled her close to plant a kiss on her cheek. "I know," he whispered.

Friar leaned in close to Divine, and pointed to the Lenora in the room. "She's the one who disappeared all her people."

"I can hear you," Lenora snapped. "I'm going to fix things without her help."

Rex, stifling a yawn, said, "All we mean is that Lenny is causing all this dysfunction or whatever it is because of her change—it happens in one way or another to all Bradley family folk no matter how far back or where the lines deviate. She's different though, and we don't know how to deal with what's going on with her or how to stop the craziness. But for certain, she's the one who is not only the disease here, but also the cure."

"Well said," offered Divine. "It's not that you can't figure it out, Lenora, it's that you need a live specimen to compare your data streams. A piece of Lenny's DNA might help move things along."

Both Frankie and Lenora were nodding, knowing that they did indeed need Lenny's DNA to match it with their findings. Then they could work backwards from there.

"Okay, so how can we get some of her DNA? Anyone here have any small bit of her on them?" asked Lenora.

Frankie cleared his throat. "Well … the only way to really get her DNA is to get her back here or us back to her—unless one of you have any of her hair or something like that on you."

"No," said Rex. "She's more likely to have *our* hair on her since we're the ones who shed."

Lenora just shook her head. "I can't believe this is happening," she mumbled.

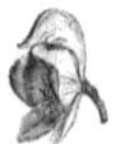

"Well, that could have gone differently," Lenora said as she pulled herself up from the floor and went to kneel by Charlotte. "Are you all right?" she said to her, taking her hand.

Charlotte looked spent. Her luxurious hair was limp, its shine replaced by dull strands. Her cheeks were sunken and her eyes drained of life. She nodded at Lenora and tears fell from her eyes. "My boys, my cubs...gone because of that monster. It lied to them and it took their souls. I watched them die. It nearly had me, too."

"I know," whispered Lenora, and she leaned in to pull the frail woman to her. "I'm gonna get it, Charlotte. I'll make it pay. I promise you." There was no longer a distance between them. She could feel herself understanding the pain of another so much more clearly now. Was this a power, too? It was one she could do without at the moment. But no, this was her and nothing more. It was how she reacted to those she felt a connection to. The thought startled her, since her prior feelings when dealing with Charlotte had been fear and intimidation. But when those two heavy emotions were pushed aside, there was a link to the woman that was tight. She shook her head and frowned. Life was complicated, that was for sure.

Margo tapped on her shoulder. "How about you? Are *you* all right?" Then she turned her head slightly, motioning to the people still on the basement floor looking scared and surprised. "And what about them?"

Lenora helped Charlotte up with the help of Margo on the other side. The three women made their way the few steps to the other side of the basement to the people who, though seeming afraid, looked to be unhurt.

"My name is Lenora Dale; this is my best friend in the world, Margo, and my new mom, Charlotte. We're sorry she's naked right now." Margo smiled and lifted her hand in a wave. Charlotte just looked at Lenora with a blank stare and tilted her head as if she'd not heard correctly.

Lenora continued. "I have a story to tell you before we can decide what to do next. It won't be easy to hear." She launched into the tale of her situation, talking about the love of her life, Frankie, the Bradley family (even though she could feel the tension in Charlotte as she told family secrets), the second Lenora, the portals, her powers, the basement cloud, their involvement, even Ned the Gorilla. At the end, everyone in the room remained dead quiet.

Then one young woman about Lenora's age stood. Everyone looked to her and waited in hope for her words, for she was one of the people who had been working on the experiment in the past. "I want to go home now," she said, and then began crying.

The people then all began talking and showing anguish resulting from their ordeal. It was obvious to the three women watching that none of the people understood what had happened and that they found Lenora's story...not without insanity.

"That went well," whispered Margo.

"Let's get everyone upstairs, get some food in them, clothes for those of us needing them, and try to make some sense of our next steps." Still supporting Charlotte's weight, Lenora looked at the drained woman at her side. "I don't know what to do about you getting your strength back, Charlotte. When my power kicked in, I was almighty! Do you think if you turn, that will bring your health back more quickly?"

"You've been watching too much television," replied Charlotte in a raspy whisper. "Still, they do get some of it right, and yes, that should help me. Let me go someplace in private to change."

Lenora and Margo helped her up the stairs with all fourteen people following them. Once they were all in the living room, Lenora nodded for Margo to take Charlotte into her bedroom. There were no words; each understood that this would be where Charlotte would come back to her full power and self—not that anyone really wanted the old Charlotte, but the women knew they needed her prowess if they were to find the rest of their group and stop the chompers. Lenora sighed hard, wondering where Frankie was and if the cat and two wolves were safe.

"What now?" said a man from the group of fourteen. His voice held an edge of panic, and he was not far from losing his wits. Everyone looked from him to Lenora.

"Do they have pizza delivery in 1944?" she said, smiling at everyone. She then picked up her phone and called in an order.

And then Frankie appeared, a bewildered look on his face.

"It's Franklin!" called out one of the fourteen. "And he's a ghost like we were."

"Not entirely," said Lenora, pushing through the crowd. "He can move around; you all were stuck in my basement."

"Lenora!" cried Frankie. "I'm back. Again."

"We see that," said Charlotte, now fully recovered and wearing one of Lenora's maxi dresses. "And I can finally see you. So are you a ghost or not a ghost?"

Lenora threw her arms around him, shocking him. "I've been so worried about you!"

Charlotte grabbed Lenora's arm and pulled her back. "No time, girl." And to Frankie, "Where are the three Bradley family members? Are they alive?"

"Oh, very much so," said Frankie. "You can all see me now? This wolf woman has a good question. What am I, and am I here and there or just here?"

"I just want to go home," said the girl who had posed that sentiment before. Another of the group patted her on the back.

Frankie became adamant now. "My Lenora needs this Lenora's DNA. It's the only way we can identify these portals and understand them enough to stop them. We think it has to do with your change, Lenny."

Lenora frowned. "Lenny?"

"Yes, it was confusing having two Lenoras and talking about both of you. So we used Margo's endearment of Lenny for you and the full name for my Lenora." Frankie was matter of fact and did not see the crushed look on Lenora's face at his choice of words.

She quickly pushed back her feelings. "DNA. Why? What does that have to do with anything?"

"Your DNA is changing, and with it, the air around you is changing to accommodate these powers you are displaying. We have to understand your DNA to get to the bottom of this," said Frankie.

"You can do that back in the 1940s?" asked Charlotte.

"Well...not exactly, but we have some ideas," he said. He cringed slightly with uncertainty. "Lenora said we need it, so we need it."

"Well, if *she* says so, it must be true," Lenny said with a twinge of sarcasm.

Frankie only nodded, the sarcasm lost on him. "And Charlotte, I can tell you that Rex, Divine, and Friar are fine. They lack class, but they're fine."

"Now who's sarcastic," whispered Charlotte to Lenora. "Give him the DNA and send him back in time, girl."

Margo disappeared into the bedroom and seconds later came out with one of Lenora's toothbrushes. "Here," she said, handing it to Frankie. "This should do for the DNA."

"Yes, that will do fine." He turned back to Lenora. "Now how do I get back?"

"Okay," began Lenora as she paced in front of the group. "Frankie, Charlotte, Margo, and I will go back to Divine's place in the woods. We'll go through the portal there. That's how we got there in the first place. If the worst happens and we end up with chompers, I'll suck the air out of the room again."

Margo was now frowning. "You think that will work a second time? And if you suck the air out of the room and there's no place for us to escape to, how do we survive?"

Charlotte just raised her eyebrows.

"It's a pickle," said a short, bald man from the fourteen.

Lenora turned to the television and switched it on, then took forty dollars from her purse and handed it to the man. "When someone knocks on the door with your pizzas, give him this in payment. Then just relax, eat, and watch TV until we get back. There are drinks in the fridge."

Charlotte said, "A field trip, then."

The three women and Frankie left the fourteen behind.

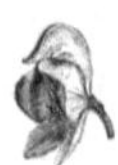

Outside the portal room in the hall at Divine and Friar's hideaway in the woods, everyone was on edge. They knew that what they were about to try might not work. It wasn't that they were particularly afraid of showing up at another location via the portal; it was more the fear of ending up at a chomper location. Was there just one of those that was hooked to several places, or were there others they could be dropped into? Had Lenora solved that issue by sucking the air out of the room at the one location in her basement, thereby dispensing the problem at Charlotte's home, too? Or were there more portals that they would need to deal with?

Frankie was particularly nervous because he'd never traveled through a portal. He'd always just appeared and disappeared—no one understood his comings and goings and what he truly was: ghost or some other anomaly unexplored.

Margo spoke up in a whisper, "I could shut it down—banish it—I think, but that wouldn't help us get to where we need to be."

"Why didn't you mention that before at my place?" remarked Charlotte. She was scowling and hanging back.

"I'm sorry," Margo began. "I was so scared of all that was happening...and besides, that was a real evil one. I'm not sure I'm that good."

Everyone just nodded, knowing this was likely an understatement when it came to chompers.

"Just hang on to that banishment thought," yelled Lenora, forgetting she was the only one hearing the rapid winds of the portal beyond the door. "We may need it sooner than later." Grasping the doorknob, she said, "Okay, gang, each of you hold on to each other and Margo to me. Margo, don't get disconnected. It would never do for us to end up in different places."

"Big yes to that," offered Charlotte.

"What about me?" asked Frankie. "Will it take me, or—" Just then he zapped out of sight.

"Well, that answers that," said Margo. "At least he has the toothbrush for your DNA sample."

Lenora was shaking, though. She'd not expected to lose him like that, and she was thinking the worst. What if... Charlotte leaned forward around Margo and touched Lenora's arm. "It will be all right, little one. He apparently has been coming and going this way for quite some time and has no better idea than we do about what is happening. I know you feel for him, but you must collect yourself now."

Lenora just nodded; then she shouted to Margo, "Tell me how you close a portal in the ghost world you live in. Come close to my ear so I can hear you over the noise."

Margo just glanced at Charlotte and shrugged since neither woman could hear anything. Margo leaned toward Lenora and spoke into her ear for a minute or so, with Lenora finally nodding her understanding.

"Just in case I need to do it," Lenora yelled. "At least I'll have some idea of what to do. Maybe. But we can't shut anything down until everyone is back into their rightful places." She paused at that, her own internal words pumping sorrow to all parts of her brain. This of course meant that Frankie would and should be in his own time. Away from her. Her love, gone. She hung her head.

"Snap out of it, my friend," coaxed Margo gently into her ear. "Let's get this done. We have to see if we can go through this thing and fix this craziness."

With that, Lenora jerked open the door and called out, "Hold on to me and to each other! Charlotte, you better turn now, and Margo, grab her dress so she has something to wear when she comes back to human!"

In an instant all of them saw the swirling green portal of wind. Margo held onto Charlotte's fur with a terrified look on her face but hung on nonetheless, and they were pulled into the mass behind Lenora. Seconds later they stood in the alley outside Lenora's frame shop, startled and shaking.

"Step back from the spot we're in," yelled Lenora, though the portal and sound were gone now.

All three women stepped back, and Margo, looking around, asked, "Where are we?"

A small spinning air cloud whipped Charlotte back to human and Margo handed the naked woman her dress. "What a way to travel, eh?" said Margo, still shaking. "I can't believe I've actually done it. I'm livin' the dream."

"Nightmare," remarked Charlotte, pulling on her dress. "Not to repeat the question, but where are we?"

Lenora was frowning and pacing. "We're nowhere. We're outside the frame shop where I work. In the alley.

We were dropped here once before from the past. This doesn't help anything at all." She looked up to the heavens, "Frankie! Where are you?" But there was no answer. "Now what?" she said softly to herself. "Where to now?"

Suddenly, they heard a strange tornado-like sound, as though a freight train were about to run them down. They stood back even farther from where they'd dropped into the alley and clung to each other. Something was about to happen.

Then in an instant, there stood Rex, Friar, Divine, Frankie, and the duplicate Lenora. They'd materialized right in front of them. Everyone had wide eyes and mouths. They were all now in one location.

Lenora's home was filled to the brim with scientists, Bradley wolves and cat, a ghost hunter, Frankie, and two Lenoras. It was a fine place for just her, but put twenty people inside and it was impossible to move, let alone come up with a plan. Everyone had something to say, and most of it had nothing to do with what Lenora, Margo, and the Bradley family knew to be the crux of the mystery. It was Lenora's change that was causing all the havoc.

Once name and job titles had been exchanged and everyone understood the Lenny/Lenora identification process, the easel with paper and marker was put to the front with Margo at the helm. Again, they listed what they knew, and it was finally understood that the portals and Lenora were probably responsible and that her DNA was the only thing that could control their movements (desired or not) through the multiverse.

Lenny sat back on the arm of her sofa just watching the process of scientists working. Frankie was real this time. Everyone saw him. He was not a ghost. He'd come through the portal just like the others. It was so odd, though, that those from the time past did not lose their clothes like those going back from the future. Another mystery. But it was clear that Frankie was uncomfortable having both her and the "other one" in the same room. And "she" kept sending cold glances her way as if she were encroaching on a territory that was only hers. Lenny did not like Lenora. And she did not want her around Frankie. But at the same time, she knew that this Frankie was not her ghost Frankie—this one belonged in the past to her counterpart. It was as though his personality had changed. He belonged with her. *So where does that leave me?*

The discussion was now centering on the chompers. Everyone was afraid of these creatures, and their nature was the topic of discussion. Charlotte told her story, her demeanor no longer the overpowering alpha female of an important wolf pack, but a mother of a family torn from the vestiges of cruel time. She told how the creatures had come as a cloudy dark smoke and smothered her cubs, feeding delicious fantasies to their brains, all the while sucking their life force—their souls—from their bodies. This happened little by little, until they succumbed and were left discarded on the floor. The fourteen told stories as well, because they'd passed through the creatures and were put into a holding pattern in Lenora's basement. It was as though something intervened and pulled them from the creatures. They could hear them behind the strange door in the basement, and they could even feel on some level the power and life being taken from those who fell victim in that place. It was not only this earth that deposited people there, but beings from many places in the multiverse ended up there to be eaten and thrown away as refuse. They were witnesses.

Frankie spoke up. "I understand it now. After hearing your accounts, it's obvious the chompers are drawn to places where an excess of electromagnetic power is evident. Lenny's change has to do with electromagnetically built energy waves, and anything inside the particular universe having matching energy is drawn to her. The creatures are drawn to places she frequents or that hold any kind of significant energy once they have identified the source." He paused and looked at her. "We were working with high ranges of electromagnetics, so you drew us to you through the multiverse, as well as all our scientists who happened to be there when we turned our machine on to test." Then he smiled at her.

Lenny's heart melted at his smile, but that melt was dislodged when the other Lenora stepped in front of her, glaring. "So this is all *your* fault," she said. "You made all this happen and you've killed people, and kidnapped them, and stranded them along other timelines in places we can't reach. There's no telling who else is victimized that we don't even know about because of you."

Lenny's back went up and she could feel her skin begin to pull up its armor. She could feel her whole body tingling.

Frankie stepped between them. "Okay, that's enough, you two."

Lenny replied with venom in her tone. "I never said or did anything. It's not like I can control what's happening to me. I still don't understand it." Then, moving into Lenora's personal space, she said, "How dare you come into my home, in my time, and attack me, when you were working with electromagnetics and actually *knew* about its properties."

It was evident a fight was brewing, but only a few knew that it was more about desire for Frankie than the situation they all found themselves in. Frankie knew, though, and this further infuriated Lenny. Why didn't he take sides? He certainly would not choose a harsh woman like "her" as his lover when *she* was available—someone who could offer him desire and affection suiting any need he might have.

But she could see the small glances he threw in *the other woman's* direction. He had taken sides after all. And it was not with her. Yes, she could tell this new physical version of Frankie had feelings for her, but things were not the same as when he was the ghost Frankie. He was now seeing that they were two different women, whereas before she knew he'd seen them as two parts of one woman. She sighed inwardly, knowing it was time to move on, to forget him. It was time to solve their mysteries, save the world, and get on with their rightful lives in their rightful places.

Margo suddenly raised her arms to wave. "Hey, now, eyes on me, peeps. I have an idea."

The room went silent, all intent on Margo.

"I've been sitting here thinking and trying to figure out what exactly is holding us back here. I've listened to all of your speculations—science and inherited energies and whatever else you've all been talking about over my head. And we've all agreed that it comes back to Lenny and her getting her new powers—thank you very much Bradley family of horrors." She looked at Charlotte, Rex, Friar, and Divine. "No offense."

Charlotte rolled her eyes, but the men just nodded.

"Anyway, the idea then, is to find out what Lenny knows," said Margo.

Charlotte sighed, but it was a sound of aggravation. "We already know the girl knows nothing. That's the problem. Or one of them at least."

Lenny wrinkled her nose. "Sitting right here, ya know."

Margo just smiled at Lenny. "Ignore them. How about I hypnotize you? I'm certified for doing it for alien abduction, and it will be easy to change it up a bit to fit this."

Frankie snapped his fingers. "Yes, that might work!" Then he frowned. "Alien abduction?" His Lenora chuffed her doubt.

"What would you gain by doing it?" asked Lenny. "How does that help us?"

Margo went on, "If I'm right in my thinking, I believe that you have these recessed powers that are to all hit full force when you turn twenty-five, but that down deep somewhere in your DNA you know what they are, why they are, and how they work. Knowing what we're dealing with will be the key to figuring out what to do about it."

Lenny stood, her eyes wide with excitement, and the others in the room all began talking at once. This was a good idea.

Minutes later the group was situated around Lenny who was relaxed in an automatic reclining chair. They'd darkened the room with drawn curtains, flicked on the air conditioning fan for soft background white noise, and settled down to hear what Margo would bring from Lenny's subconscious.

Margo began by asking Lenny to close her eyes and relax. She took her through relaxation exercises via visualization so comforting that the entire group become drowsy and receptive. Down, down, Margo took Lenny to a relaxing seascape where she sat with her at the water's edge.

Lenny yawned widely and just gazed out over the crystal clear water of the lake near her frame shop. The day was warm, and the wooden bench she sat on held the heat from the morning sun. Birds were calling out in their beautiful voices as if to welcome her to their world of soaring wings and freedom. This was the kind of day that brought a person great strength because the energy of the sun, of the water, of the surroundings as a whole gave freely, and she was able to participate in a give-and-take that nourished her soul.

It was strange there were no runners on the path by the water or children playing on the vast lawns, but it felt reassuring just the same. It was then that she noticed that Frankie sat on the bench with her.

"Hello, Doll," he said to her softly. "I'm right here with you. You can do this."

"Do what?" she asked, then added, "Please don't call me Doll anymore, dearest."

"I'm sorry, Lenny. I'll try harder not to do that," he said, putting his hand on her arm. "Do you know why we're here?"

Lenny frowned. At her peripheral vision she thought she could see someone—Margo, perhaps—but definitely others listening in as though she were a speaker of many truths that they desired to know. *I must be mistaken. It's just me here. And my love, Frankie.* She slid closer to him on the bench, took his hand from her arm, and placed it on the side of her face to feel his warmth and his love for her. He touched her face gently and then drew her into his arms. She allowed the embrace and returned it by putting her arms around his neck. Looking into each other's eyes, they both knew at the same time that a kiss was necessary to seal this encounter. Their lips met, and the soft touch of mouth to mouth brought out a fever in Lenny that she wanted to hold in her heart forever.

It was then that she heard a rustling or a commotion of whispers behind her. Someone was angry, it seemed. There was angst in the sounds she heard. This pulled her back from Frankie's embrace...and he was suddenly gone.

"He does come and go quickly," she said out loud.

Then Margo was there on the bench.

"Where did you come from?" she asked her friend. "Frankie was here. Now he's not."

"Yes, I know," answered Margo. "Let's keep him gone for a bit, shall we? Let's just you and me talk, my friend. We need to get to the bottom of some things. Do you understand?"

Lenny sighed and looked back out over the sparkling water. "No. Not really. I just want to relax here a while."

"I know," comforted Margo, "but there will be plenty of time to relax soon. Let's talk about your powers, Lenny. Do you know what I'm asking you?"

Lenny nodded. "Of course. They are coming in lickety-split, aren't they?" There was a smile in her tone of voice. "Frankie brings them out of me. Dear Frankie."

More rustling sounds came from behind them and Lenny looked around. "Who is back there, Margo?"

"Oh, well, not to worry," she answered. "That's being handled." Then to someone else: "That's being handled, right?"

Silence.

Lenny looked back at Margo. "My powers are for the good of the multiverse, you know. Gorilla Ned should have never crossed me that first day. That's when I first used them."

"Yes, but you didn't understand them then. Do you know what they are now and what they do?" asked Margo.

"I do." There was confidence in Lenny's voice. "The protective powers of my body armor are evident. It protects me. That kind of protection is needed for moving through the multiverse to correct the balances in energy."

Margo frowned. "What? I don't understand."

"Everyone will soon enough—when I turn twenty-five. I'll be called upon to disperse extra energy that becomes destructive or that invites the evil energy stealers." She was nodding as if this was the clearest concept in the world.

"You mean the chompers?" asked Margo. "You will be traveling through the multiverse stomping out chompers?"

"That's only part of it," answered Lenny. "Frankie and I will restore balance through his electromagnetic experiments. The chompers are just an evil consequence of having access to that energy. I can take care of them by closing their portals wherever they show up. You taught me that, dear Margo. I know how to do it because I can combine your technique with my control of the energies. They kill life. They must be banished. And those who would abuse normal biological energy for less than safe purposes must be balanced."

More confusion was in the air behind them and Lenny looked back over her shoulder. "They make it difficult to relax, you know."

"Yes, they will be quiet now. They are excited about what you're saying and asking me questions to ask you."

Lenny merely nodded and looked back to the water.

Margo continued, "Will you be getting any other powers? And how do we get Frankie and Lenora's scientists—and them—back to their time?"

Lenny tilted her head. "It's not a matter of sending them back to their time. We are not on portions of the same timeline. We are in two different universes within the multiverse. I have all my powers, just not the full strength. I'll be drinking more water to help that along. Water sustains my powers and gives them a boost. I have enough power to settle things here though." She paused. "But I don't want to. I don't want to send Frankie away. He needs to be here with me."

The rustling commotion and whispers became persistent behind them, and though Lenny shifted her eyes, she did not look back. "I'm serious about this. Frankie stays. He loves me, not her."

Margo began again, "Lenny, listen carefully, the Frankie that you know is not from our world—he belongs in another world. I know you have feelings for him, but if we don't close down the bad portals and send the scientists, Lenora, *and* Frankie home, it will upset the space time continuum."

"*Star Trek*? Really, Margo?" Lenny laughed then. "Look, I don't make this decision lightly. Frankie wants to stay here with me. We have work to do."

More background commotion.

Margo, speaking words very cautiously now, began again. "Lenny, he's from another world, and their energies are not balanced with them gone. He can't stay here. He doesn't have your powers. You'd be killing a lot of people by allowing their world to remain in a...uhmmm...unbalance of energy."

Lenny remained quiet, but as she stared out at the water, a tear fell down her cheek from her welled eyes. Knowing what was right did not mean it would be easy to accomplish or be without the pain of loss. "I know you're right."

"How do you control the energy, Lenny?" Margo asked. "I know how the portals will be closed, but how do you balance energy? Do you suck the excess out of a place like you do air out of a room?"

Lenny looked back at her. "No, of course not. That's just a control method to keep me in charge. I will soon know how to keep my own air, while taking away that of others."

Margo cringed. "That sounds like evil scientist kinda scary stuff, my friend."

Lenny smiled at her. "No, just chomper mentality. They are called many things throughout the multiverse—thought forms, vitality depleters, monsters … you know. They take control of a person's inner being and steal it away. They don't always kill; sometimes they just weaken and weaken an entity until the only thing left is anguish and debilitating unrest. They cause wars. I would never use the air drain on a positive being."

Margo's eyes were wide and her eyebrows were raised. "So when you're twenty-five you're gonna be like a Wonder Woman or some super hero."

"Odd to think of it that way," she said and stretched, "but that's right, in a way." She paused. "I wonder if I'll remember all this when you wake me up. Can you make sure I remember it?"

"Of course," said Margo. "What is the first thing we should do though, when you wake, Lenny? How do we get the people back to their multiverse?"

"All I have to do is let go, and wish them back—for lack of another descriptive word." Her voice was monotone, flat and cold. "It will mean that I will never see Frankie again. It will mean I've given up on love."

Margo tried to console her. "Lenny, remember he's not from here. You weren't meant to be with him. And I'm sorry, but he loves the other you from the other universe. He's not meant for you."

"I know," was all she said.

Then she woke from her trance.

Chapter Twelve

THE FIRST THING LENORA NOTICED when she woke from her hypnotic trance was that she felt fabulous—more rested than she'd felt in quite some time, and at least since all the portal and change problems. The next thing she noticed was that the only people in the room with her were Margo, Charlotte, Rex, Divine, and Friar.

"What happened to everyone else?" she asked, looking around.

They all looked at each other and then Rex said, "Well, they were here one minute, and the next they were gone. You know how that goes."

"I went down in the basement," added Divine, "and I didn't get the feeling that anyone was in a cloud down there. So they're not there."

"No," said Charlotte, "and there's no...spark in the air like before. Now that it's gone, I recognize that ever since that Frankie and those workers were here, there was a spark to the air. It had become so normal, that I no longer even recognized the difference. It became...life."

"I think you let them go back, Lenny, when you were in your hypnotic state—all of them," said Margo. "It was the right thing to do. I know it was hard."

Lenora waved her hand at Margo to dismiss the distress of the situation. "You were right. It wasn't Frankie's place here with me. And, of course, the others." To Charlotte she said, "I really need family help, Charlotte. I understand the powers now, but controlling them or using them... well, I just don't have a clue."

"And, it's also true that we don't know how to help you," said Charlotte, "but we will stand by you and help you with the energy balance of the worlds if we can. Rex will never leave your side."

Rex grimaced. "Not that I don't want to be at her side, dear stepmom, but that's not how Lenny's and my relationship works. We're friends. We're siblings of a sort. We're *not* the dynamic duo of superhero days gone wrong." He turned to Lenora. "We are here for you, though. All of us."

Lenny nodded again brushing away a tear, but not one of happiness for being welcomed to a family. It was the loss of the only man she'd ever had such warm feelings for. She'd sacrificed her love, but nothing could be done about it. She sighed. "I need to rest. Then we have to get to the task of closing portals."

Everyone agreed.

Margo stood in front of the small group of portal closers. They didn't carry weapons, and they weren't dressed like military or super heroes. They were just themselves trying to make sense of what their trainer was saying.

"The way I see it," Margo was saying, "there is one really big positive to this as well as one really big danger. The positive is that we have Lenny, who has the ability to control the energy around these swirling things. The bad and dangerous news is that we have Lenny, who has the ability to control the energy around these things. When she's around, people get sucked to different places. I don't think it's safe for any one of us to try to close a portal with her around." She paused. "And we probably can't do it without her."

Charlotte said, "Well, ghost gal, then what do you propose? You can't have it both ways."

The men were nodding. Lenora remained quiet, needing to trust her friend's knack for the paranormal solutions.

"What I'm suggesting," said Margo, pulling three pendulums from her ghost hunting case, "is that we break up into three teams: Rex and Charlotte; Divine and Friar; me and Lenny." She handed a pendulum to Charlotte and another to Divine. "Have you used these before? Do you understand dowsing?"

Lenora was nodding, but mostly there were just blank stares.

Lenora offered, "Dowsing has been around a very long time. You've heard of people finding water wells by holding a v-shaped branch, and it eventually pulls downward when above a well? This is like that, only we use crystals or metals on a chain. Some people use religious symbols, or you can even use that crested necklace around your neck, Rex." Rex looked down and grasped the gemstone in wonder. She continued, "The energy in the atmosphere and from inside us then reaches out to find what we need. The pendulum will either pull toward the thing you want, or start to turn in a circle. Or it could move back and forth. Each person has their own connection to the pendulum, and it moves according to that. So you have to ask it what a 'yes' looks like, what a 'no' looks like—any question you consider asking...within reason."

Margo took one and stood near the basement door. She became very quiet and then said, "Now I'm concentrating on what I want to know about—in this case, where a portal is." When it senses what I'm looking for, it will pull in that direction or I can walk around until I can feel a pull. It's real gentle at first and then stronger as you get nearer to your desire and used to using and feeling the pendulum's energy."

Lenora said, "Kinda like the hot-cold game kids play."

"Charlotte's team and Divine's team can go searching for the portals and make notes of what they find. I'd say start at Charlotte's house—we know of the one in the attic, but maybe there are more. And Divine's place in the woods. We already know about the basement here and the place near Lenny's frame shop." Margo seemed to have a plan in place, but she cautioned, "No one should really team up closely with Lenny, though. Even me. When she's around, these portals whip us into them. We don't want any more moving around the multiverse until we understand more of what she's supposed to become. And we don't want to drag any more people here. Agreed?"

Everyone was happy to agree and not travel anymore to foreign worlds or meet new uninvited "friends."

"Will we be able to see the portals now, do you think?" asked Friar.

"I don't think so. That means you have to be super careful. It could be that even having Lenny thinking about this stuff could have her sending us all over the place."

Rex raised his eyes. "Point taken."

As they were talking, something was happening to Margo's pendulum. The gem was pulling up and up toward the basement door. Everyone stood transfixed looking at it, now nearly horizontal.

"See?" said Margo. "It's pointing toward the basement where the portals are. Of course there might be one or even two down there—we don't really know what Lenny did to the chompers' door. They went somewhere, or they could be down there right behind a door none of us can see."

"Okay," said Rex. "So we find 'em and you two close 'em."

"Yes," said Margo, "in theory. Why don't you all practice here before heading out."

With that everyone began to work with the pendulums to see if they could get the same results as Margo at the basement door. All were pleased to find that the pendulums were good tools for them. It would seem that wolf—and cat—energy was larger than life. They were all impressed with each other, and for a while the atmosphere was light and encouraging as they learned to identify the pendulums' energies.

"Okay," said Lenora after the others left. "Let me get this straight. All I have to do to close these things is to focus on them, turn them into pieces of fabric in my mind that have a slit in the middle with swirling light shining through—kinda like stuffing all the tornado stuff inside— and then stitch it up with a big sewing needle from my mind. That sews the thing shut and keeps everything on the other side of it away from us."

"Right," said Margo, "again, in theory. I'm thinking that no one can see these things unless you're with them and maybe not even then as you know, and so they really can't do it. I mean I used to do this, but not for things as powerful as this. And I could never physically see them. It's an in-the-mind kind of thing."

Lenora shrugged. "Maybe you did master it, but you just didn't know it."

"Maybe," she answered. "I know that what I was doing, though, was finding the ones that were opened by strong spirits—the negative ones that stay around to haunt people. The idea was to control them and then drive them out—keep them behind the curtain so they couldn't come out anyplace else. Who knew that portals were around like these multiverse ones?"

Lenora thought for a few seconds. "Ya know, I think they are all the same, Margo. You've been working with the multiverse all along with your haunted people and places. It just took my powers to make them visible in the here and now. Not a good thing, obviously. There are probably all kinds of portals with all kinds of things in them—some good like our counterparts or long-lost relatives, and others like the chompers, or demons, or other evil things we've heard legends about over the years."

"Wow, maybe even Bigfoot," said Margo. "You just summed up my life. My whole belief system has changed now."

"Mine, too," said Lenora with a sigh. "So what are you going to do? Just supervise so you don't get sucked in when I do this stuff?"

"Yeah, I'm gonna be a hall monitor. Let everyone else do the work, and I'll take notes." Margo laughed, but Lenora could hear the discomfort in her voice. She was hanging back to make sure there was someone left behind to tell the story if things went wrong. A last person to make things right.

"Okay," said Lenora, "let's get to it. I'm going into the basement."

"Should we use the rope idea again? That worked the first time," suggested Margo, grabbing the rope that had been thrown behind the sofa.

"No," said Lenora. "I don't need it now. Somehow I just know that." She paused and held up her arm. "Look, the armor is here. I'm good to go."

Except...when they opened the basement door, there was soft sobbing coming from the far corners of the room out of their sight from the top of the stairs. It sounded like Frankie.

Lenora pushed Margo gently back. "You stay here. I'm going down. He needs me."

"Remember, it could be a chomper trick, Lenny," said Margo. "You don't want to get caught like Charlotte did. They almost got you once. I won't be able to suck any air out for you like you did for her. And Frankie's not the crying type as far as I could see!"

But Lenora had already started down the stairs, the sounds of her love drawing her along with little thought of surrounding dangers. A little voice in the back of her mind said *stupid move, don't go into the basement!* But—as heroines are wont to do—she ignored it and pushed it back. No time for fear now.

Franklin and Lenora were arguing once the fourteen scientists had left their offices to get back to their homes. Three had even quit their jobs. Of course, this was understandable considering what they'd all just been through.

"Look, I'm not saying that you had any special feelings for her; it just felt that way to me. And you have to know that she is not me. *I'm* me. Look at all we've been through together for you to just up and start caring for someone else who just looks like me, but isn't." Lenora was fighting back an impulse to throttle Franklin, because he just stood there not saying a word. He looked like a hurt dog, and that made her even angrier. She'd done nothing to warrant this. After all this time, one expected a relationship as close as theirs to be stable and lasting. This kind of thing just was not normal.

"You're not going to say anything at all to me?" she demanded. "Nothing?" She paused but not really long enough for him to answer. "Well, that's fine then. Go back to her, and see if she can do any better with this whole mess." With that she walked out, slamming the door so hard it rocked on the hinges.

Franklin slumped down in his chair. How could he begin to tell his Lenora all that he was feeling and the confusion that gave him not a minute of peace? The Lenora in the future was so appealing, and it was difficult for him to tell the two women apart in many ways. Here, she was a no-nonsense, clear as a bell, to-the-point, and in-control woman. She was strong and had solid opinions. She took care of business. The Lenora from the other time had a softer side. She was willing to listen to all points of view before making a decision. And when she did make that decision, you could bet that her heart was in it as much as her mind. It was nice. The softness to her nature made her more attractive.

It wasn't that he didn't love his Lenora. He did. Frantically. Without question. But he'd seen the hurt in the other woman's eyes, and it felt to him as though he was killing a part of her by not recognizing her in the same way in this timeline.

Without warning, tears began to flow down his face and sobs escaped into the room. He tried to hold them back, but once started, he couldn't stop. His own weakness was infuriating to him, and mixing that with the guilt he felt just made things worse. That was when he disappeared from the room.

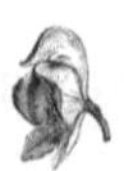

Lenora, now in the basement, had her arms around the sobbing Frankie, who suddenly turned from a ghostly figure on the floor in the corner to a real person—someone she could touch. Her heart ached as she saw his tears, and she leaned in closer to hold him tighter. He held her back.

"What's wrong, dearest?" she whispered as she stroked his hair. "Why are you back? What's happened?"

Frankie took in a deep breath and sat back from her, wiping his tears. "Sorry for the waterworks. Everyone was back. Everything was fine. We'd done it—at least getting the scientists home. Then my Lenora and I fought. Next thing I know, I'm here … in your arms. What does that mean, Doll?"

"I don't know," said Lenora "I guess we are still connected, and since we both were in a type of mourning, it pulled you back here. My personal electromagnetic energy is getting stronger every day. And that infernal experiment of yours is mucking up the whole thing." She paused, stood, and offered him a hand up. He took it.

She began again, this time turning away from him. "Frankie, I know things are complicated in your life with two of us." She pointed to herself and then threw her arm up to indicate some other person. "As much as I would like to have you here, you have to go back. You have to stop the experiments until after I'm twenty-five and have my full powers so that I can protect the universe here. You have to go back to her." She fought to hide the catch in her throat, for what she said was not what she wanted. "It's too dangerous for this to go on any longer. You have to forget me, and I have to forget you. And I have to close all the portals that I can find, wherever they show up."

Then there was silence. Lenora wondered if this was as difficult for him as it was for her. He likely was quiet because of the incredible pain involved in splitting them apart—away from each other for all time. She turned to console him.

He was gone. The basement was empty except for a spark of electromagnetic feeling in the air. A tear fell down her face as she pictured the fabric of time—a slit vertically in the air with the tornado portal behind it. She began to stitch up the tear, more and more weeping touching her very soul. No one would come through this portal again.

She called up to Margo, "The portal in the front of the basement is closed, and Frankie's gone. Now I'm going for the chomper one at the back of the room.

"Be careful," warned Margo. "I still think the rope might be a good touch."

"No," replied Lenora in a normal voice. "I'm not going to open this one to sew it shut. I'm going to use enforced energy cement that I'm creating in my mind. Those suckers won't get through it." Then she closed her eyes and pictured a magical cement wall going up across the back basement wall, trapping the chompers. In the distance, she could hear their cries of horror and fear as they were tucked away inside a supernatural fortress. "Well," said Lenora, brushing her hands against each other like a job well done, "that's that."

Calling up to Margo, she said, "Call the others to see how they're doing locating these things. It's time to shut this all down."

The easel was set up at the frame shop's storefront window and Lenora's paints were scattered on a table to the side. She wore a colorful smock to keep the excess paint from her clothes. Her hair was loose and she wore no makeup. She still showed up for work each day she was scheduled, and she went through the motions of daily life. But that life now held no luster. Each day was just another to get through before the next one came along. Then she had to get through that one, too.

The scene she was painting had been etched into her mind since the moment Frankie had disappeared for the final time. They'd closed all the portals with more ease than felt comfortable, but the Bradleys and Margo seemed happy with how things turned out. They felt no worry about other such things. They were done. The disaster had been thwarted. Only Rex seemed to recognize her pain and know that it came from a source across the multiverse. He came by every day to check on her and to invite her to dinner or some other function meant to take her mind from the agony of lost love.

Nothing worked though. So she painted. It was how she'd always taken her stress away, and it was always best to do what was familiar. The painting before her displayed a waterside scene at the lake where she'd first met Frankie. There was a bench and she'd painted herself sitting upon it, looking out at the water. The view was from behind so that all the viewer could see was her back with her hair pulled into a loose ponytail. Next to her was another figure: male, somewhat transparent, but still holding a sense of wonder and romance. He was looking at her, but only a wispy profile was shown. The lake was crystal clear with sunbeams bouncing off the water, and trees and flowers spilling out along the path where the bench sat.

"Very nice," said Rex from behind her. He gently touched her shoulder.

She didn't move to take his hand away, and she only nodded without looking back at him.

Friar stepped up next to her. "There's that infernal ghosty Frankie. You've got to get that guy outta your mind, girl."

Lenora didn't even look at him. "That's easy for a wolf to say when you have no real compulsion for staying with one individual."

Divine, sitting on a stool behind her counter, remarked, "That's not true at all. We just don't have a lot of females to choose from of our own kind. Stop being such a witch today."

Lenora shrugged. "Well, it's finished." She moved her supply table back and then tilted the easel toward the front window so that passersby could see it.

"You don't look happy at finishing it," said Rex. "What if you display it and someone wants to buy it? How will you part from it?"

Lenora shrugged again, but this time she looked directly at him. "I think I'm still holding on to him. And if someone buys this likeness of us, then they will take that time away, and it will be over for me, finally."

"Deep," said Friar.

"I don't think that's how things work," added Divine.

"Maybe not," she answered. "Maybe I won't sell it when the time comes. Maybe I will. Either way, it doesn't matter, because he's gone. And maybe he was never really here, ya know?"

They all nodded.

Rex took her hands and his eyes became bright. "Remember now, your birthday party is tomorrow, and everything will change for the better! We'll have a jolly good time at the mansion, and the whole family will be united under a strangely less-aggressive Charlotte!"

Lenora smiled weakly. "Yes, that will be nice." She looked around at them and again recognized that they were only there to cheer her up. She was not in the mood though and didn't want to ruin their lives by continually raining her pain on them. She'd begun to love them as brothers and didn't want to cause them undue stress. "I'm good, you guys. Seriously. And tomorrow will be fun. Now I have some things I have to do before closing, and you all should be on your way."

They all rose to leave, not recognizing her ploy to send them away—or maybe happy for the escape. Farewells and swift cheek kisses assaulted her and then they were out onto the street and on their way.

The painting at the window was angled so that those walking by could see it, and she could see it from the counter as well. She stood there just gazing at it and remembering the moment she'd first met Frankie. It had been so innocent. Now, here she was. Alone. The painting had a strange look, and she wasn't sure whether it was her newly received powers perceiving her real emotional pain or just the way she'd painted it. Though it was a bright sunny day in the scene, there was something gray and sad about it. Something unfinished. Something gone or missing. She sighed and began to work the closing, preparing the computer log for sales.

The bell above the door jingled, and someone walked in. Lenora looked up and sucked in her breath. Her eyes were wide and she could not move. It was Frankie.

"Hi, there," he said. He wore jeans and a sports jacket with an open-necked shirt. It did not look like her Frankie.

She nodded and managed a small smile.

"This painting in the window," he began. "Do you know the artist? Is it someone local? I've never seen anything like it. It speaks to me. You understand that, right?"

Again she nodded, and before she could speak—*if* she could speak—he started again. "I have to have it. It's like the people sitting on the bench have a story that has not been finished. You can see the heartache, but you can also see that the sun is peeking above the clouds. It's like something is about to happen. Something wonderful!"

Lenora was looking at the painting, too. She'd not looked at it the way this man was seeing it, even though these kinds of things were always well planned in her work. She looked back at him and stammered, "I-I painted it." Her voice was barely above a whisper.

"And you are?" he asked. His eyes were playful and his smile was contagious. "And has anyone ever told you what a doll you are?"

"Doll? Hmmm, I like that." She paused, surprised at how well she liked hearing him call her that. "I'm Lenora Dale," she finally answered, feeling her cheeks redden and her breath shallow. How was this possible? Doppelgangers? Still another Frankie, this time from *this* timeline? This multiverse universe? "What's your name?" she asked as calmly as she could.

"I'm Frank Malone," he said and offered his hand.

Shaking, she reached out to touch a real, solid hand—not a ghost hand—and shook it.

"I'm a professor at the university. I've been by here many times and always wanted to stop because of the paintings on display. Just never had the time. But this time. This painting. I could not walk on by. I just couldn't. Like I said, it spoke to me. It's like that's me in the painting. That's me looking at the beautiful woman.... Wait...is that woman you?"

She only smiled at him not knowing how to proceed. Then she shrugged, feeling playful now. "What do you do at the university?" she asked.

"Well," he started, "I'm working on a very interesting project dealing with electromagnetic energy and how to use it to navigate varied current phenomena in our atmosphere."

"Of course you are," she said with a newer and brighter smile. "How could you be working on anything else?"

He tilted his head in question.

"Oh, don't mind me," she said with a laugh. "Tomorrow's my birthday and I just knew that something wonderful was going to happen to me—at least I hoped it might."

His smile beamed. "And might I be that wonderful thing?"

"Of course not," she said with a coy undertone. "I meant that someone would buy my favorite painting."

"Oh," he said, disappointment in his voice.

"Maybe you'd like to come to my birthday party, tomorrow, with me," she suggested, out of character in asking out a man she didn't know. Still, she knew this Frank in a way, in another place in the multiverse.

"I'd like to, yes," he said with surprise. "I feel like I already know you. How is that possible? Very strange for me."

"Oh, you never know in this animal-like world we live in. Now. About this electromagnetic project. Have you ever thought instead of working on...maybe biometrics?" she said in a matter-of-fact tone.

"No," he said, frowning. "Why would I do that?"

Lenora sighed. "No reason...safer, maybe." *Here we go again*, she thought. But her heart felt much better now. *Much* better.

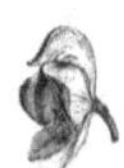

Acknowledgments

SPECIAL THANKS TO THOSE SUPPORTING ME in this book's journey: Jack Kenna, paranormal investigator and part of the *Paranormal Survivor* television program team, for discussing with me his knowledge of portals, closing them, and the energy surrounding them; the entire Chester County Paranormal Research Society for teaching me the ropes of investigation over the years; Ben and Paul Eno for educating me on the theories of multiverse as it relates to paranormal phenomena; Angela Tallent for being my cover model heroine and her photographer, Jessie Lynn Hare at Jessie Lynn Hare Photography; author Bob Davis who introduced my work to Rosemary Ellen Guiley, Rosemary and the Visionary Living team who worked on this book (including Linda Lee, Leslie McAllister, and John Cheek), Carey Massimini who shot my author photo and Meghan Schaffer who took out some hard-earned wrinkles—and to my characters, who are now quite alive in my brain and still *poofing* about.

About the Author

DINAH ROSEBERRY has been an author of both nonfiction and fiction in the paranormal field for over thirty years. She is a paranormal investigator, certified hypnotist for past-life regression and alien  abduction, and has studied and taught animal communications. A Tarot card and oracle reader for over twenty years, she has also created card decks and guidebooks that reflect her paranormal and mind/body/ spirit interests. Visit her website for more information about her titles and events: **www.roseberrybooks.com.**

Other paranormal titles by Dinah Roseberry

Ghosts of Valley Forge and Phoenixville; Cape May Haunts: Elaine's Haunted Mansion and Other Eerie Beach Tales; Spooky York, Pennsylvania; Spooky Creepy Baltimore County; The Ghost Hunters' Tool Kit; Psychic Pets: Solving Paranormal Mysteries
Animals Impacting the World; First Light Tarot; Ufo & Alien Management: A Guide to Discovering, Evaluating, and Directing Sightings, Abductions, and Contactee Experiences